Simon's Cycle Shorts

Simon A. Bever

ISBN 9781520965307

Contents

Preface

About the Author

Preface

In just over a century the humble bicycle has covered the world at a rate more rapidly than almost any other technological advance. From the poorest to richest nations, the bicycle is the brilliant product of mans ingenuity that will always be seen as the most efficient means of travel.

The humble chain driven bicycle has barely changed since it appeared towards the end of the late nineteenth century. It has seen all the other great inventions come and many of them go...but it is still here.

The great survivor has seen through revolutions, wars, famines and floods. So what if it could speak? What would it say about us? What would it say about the moments when we think we are all alone with our bicycle?

This collection of short stories gives the reader an insight into what could be the thoughts of our most enduring invention. Maybe that collection of tubes, cogs, nuts and bolts has a heart as well? Imagined moments from history, accounts of amazing rides and tender moments between man and machine; they're all here.

Enjoy the Ride!

Simon's Cycle Shorts

Tricycle Trial

"Shhh…we're going to Nan's house." Ever so quietly Sam reached up to the front door on his tip toes and undid the latch. There was a loud click as the door sprung open. He turned, put his finger to his lips and looked straight at me. "Shhh…!" For some reason he'd decided it was my fault that the latch made a noise - but my little Sam was cute so I didn't mind.

With the door wide open he took one more furtive look up the stairs before pushing me carefully out over the step and onto the path that led to the front gate. It was sunny outside, albeit a little chilly - it was only seven o'clock. After feeding himself a two-Weetabix breakfast - during which he managed to spill both the milk and the sugar across the dining table when his spoon caught the edge of the bowl - he carefully put his shoes on the wrong feet and then wriggled into his coat; it took a few goes. Finally all was good, except that there seemed to be more holes than buttons when he did it up. He shrugged unconcerned.

Sam was often up early at the weekends and came down to get his own breakfast. Usually Mum or Dad would come down too when they heard him bumping down the stairs on his bottom - he could walk down but, after his recent tumble from top to bottom, he was back to bumping down. But no one came this morning. I had been sat there in the hallway when they'd come back from the pub the night before, paid Julie for sitting Sam, and made their way up to bed. They were clearly a little drunk and Dad had that look in his eye as he followed Mum up the stairs with his hand on her bottom.

I had seen Sam's Nan a few times when she'd come to visit, but I'd not gone back to her house since I'd been given to Sam on his third birthday. I arrived at Tedder Way in the boot of Dad's car so I didn't actually know where Nan's house was.

Leaving me out in the garden and leaving the front door wide open, Sam went back to the kitchen and I heard him opening the fridge door. After scrabbling around for a minute or so he reappeared with his Pepper Pig rucksack on his back. He'd brought some supplies for the journey. Carefully pulling the front door closed behind him - it clicked again - he then climbed onto me and pedalled up to the front gate. We were off!

"Where's he taking us?" The two little wheels at the back always spoke in unison and were also a bit behind everyone else.

"He said we were going to Nan's? Don't' you two ever listen?" Saddle was as grumpy as ever - something to do with always being sat upon, I think.

"That is what the boy said - but boys never say what they mean - do they?" Front wheel always deferred to me. Well, I did hold us all together.

"Well," I was stalling. "Yes, that is what he said - but do we think he knows the way? I don't remember us ever riding to Nan's before - what do you think Pedal-Pedal?" The two of them always liked to be referred to as one.

"Whatever, whatever."

"No, we haven't ridden there, but I think he's been there in his pushchair." The handlebars were the most sensible of us all and were always able to steer us back onto the right track.

"Hmm, yes - so let's assume he knows the way." I could hear the saddle still grumbling on its post; Front wheel was keeping quiet but I could tell she wasn't happy. I think those two preferred it when we sat in the dark garage for years.

I have been part of the Simpson family for a long time - I used to be Dad's trike when he was a little boy and, when he and Mum had baby Sam, I was dragged out of Nan's garage and given to him. Nan bought me from the department store on the City Road when Dad was just a nipper. He didn't ride me a lot, but when Sam got me he told him about all the adventures we'd apparently had. Considering my age, I think I was in pretty good condition when I got handed to Sam; my red steel frame with its white handlebars and seat still shone like new, and my solid wheels with their painted-on red petal spoke-holes made it look like I'd come from the set of the Magic Roundabout. Mum had wanted to put a bell on me but Dad wouldn't have it - I don't think he liked the noise they made.

"What does she want a bell for?" Handlebars sounded uncharacteristically concerned at the prospect of a chrome Mickey Mouse bell ruining the purity of our design.

"I wouldn't be able to stand the noise - can you imagine all that ting-a-linging up and down the garden?" Front wheel was similarly against such a move; besides, Nan would never have allowed one.

Despite what they thought, a bell would have ruined the sweet sweep of the bars - I was clearly designed by someone with feeling for form and, when no one is looking, I often sneak a peak at my sweeping lines in the hallway mirror. In my opinion, I was the most beautifully designed trike ever.

The rubber tyres on my three wheels were still good - they were made solid so were never going to puncture - and my little rubber pedals still spun as well as they did the day I was made. I might have been a bit heavier than some of the other children's bikes, but I was built to last. Besides, Sam loved riding me and I still got that little thrill every time we zoomed down a slope. Feeling his little hot hands on my bars and hearing his shrill screams of delight at the wind in his mop of blonde hair always made me smile. He was a happy little boy who made everyone smile.

We'd been to the park before with Mum so at least I knew the way there - along the pavement for quite a bit before crossing at the zebra and then along Cranleigh Avenue to the Park at the end. Thankfully, it being early in the morning, there were no cars on the road when Sam drove us straight out and across the zebra without even stopping to look. I had a bit of a moment and front wheel almost had a heart attack.

"Hey look out - it's me that gets it first you know!"

Mum wouldn't have been happy with what just happened as she always told Sam to stop and wait for her. He got a proper telling off if he didn't do what Mum said. However, she wasn't there so I guess he thought that there wasn't much point in waiting.

When we got to the Park Sam seemed surprised that there was no one else there. It meant he could go on all the swings and roundabouts without having to wait for anyone else. He especially like climbing to the top of the climbing frame - it worried me as much as it did Mum whenever he hung by his little hands, but thankfully he didn't fall - who would have been there to rub his knees if he'd fallen? He also went down the slide on his tummy which he would never have done with Mum there.

"This is very dangerous you know - what will we do if he gets hurt? How will Mum know where he is?"

"He's a boy - boys always do stupid things. There's nothing we can do." Saddle was as helpful as ever.

I sat there at the edge of the rubber-floored playground area for quite a while as Sam made a point of trying every piece of equipment at least twice. I thought we would be going home after he'd played on all the pieces, but when he got back on board and started to pedal, I realised that we were going out another gate from the Park and along a road I didn't know. It was along here that we saw the man with the dog. He was wearing a big dark coat and was waiting patiently holding a lead as his Alsatian did a poo next to a lamp-post; I didn't like the look of either of them. Despite Sam smiling up at the old man, who was smoking a smelly cigarette, neither he nor the dog even looked at us as we sailed by. The dog, though, did have other things on its mind as it squatted uncomfortably and looked up into the sky over the rooftops as if trying to avoid the stink of its own doings. Sam instinctively pinched his nose as the stink wafted over us.

"Stay wide guys - we don't want to run though that!" Front wheel often forgot the little guys at the back.

Suddenly, as we were sailing down the slope caused by a dip in the pavement that marked the beginning of a driveway, I was aware of a big black bumper - we were just about to be hit by a car exiting a garden! At the last moment it came to an abrupt halt just a foot away from us. Sam didn't even seem to notice, but the old couple in the car were sat with their faces frozen in shock as we carried on our way. Looking back I could see an elderly man get out of the car and watch us pedal away up the road whilst shaking his head in disbelief.

"Is someone going to do something? This kid will be the end of us all!"

The recurring driveways got to be great fun and Sam lifted his feet as we sailed down them before deftly catching the pedals again for the up slope. After a while, the pavement turned onto a big road and we went past a row of shops. Sam didn't stop until we reached the ramp of a subway that would take us under the big road in front of us. The next thing I knew, we were careering down the slope at an alarming rate; I didn't think we would be able to stop in time for the bottom or be able to turn the sharp bend. It looked like there was nothing we could do to avoid crashing. Sam was laughing out loud as our speed increased and the air rushed through his hair. I was powerless to do anything.

Miraculously Sam managed to steer us round the sharp ninety degree bend at the bottom and into the darkness of the subway - front wheel was complaining loudly.

"Can't you stop him, you fool - he'll split my rubber!" I ignored her; what did she think I could do? Hearing his own voice echoing through the subway Sam screamed like a demon as we roared through the short tunnel and up the slope on the other side. We quickly slowed to a stop as his little legs just didn't have the power to push heavy old me up the slope. Undeterred, Sam dismounted and pushed us up. I was very proud of him. His father didn't have that sort of determination. He'd have got off at the slightest of slopes and then burst into tears until someone came to help. Sam was made of sterner stuff.

"I think we should go home now." Front wheel had her concerned voice again.

"So do we." said the rear wheels displaying a better understanding of the situation than I would have credited them with. I didn't know what to say. It surely couldn't be too far to Nan's as Mum could never walk very far before she needed a cup of tea.

"It shouldn't be long now."

"What do you know? If this goes on much further then I'm going to take a dim view of this whole caper. Sunday mornings should be for rest you know." I didn't known Saddle was religious.

"I don't know why you're so miserable - you're just sitting there - us wheels have to do all the work!"

"Pedal-pedal, pedal-pedal - who does the work?"

"Oh come on now - let's just go with it. We're having an adventure, aren't we?"

Thankfully, Sam's next turn quietened everyone down. Turning off the pavement, we went up a short passage between the houses and, before we knew it, we were in a huge field of corn. Sam was taking us across the middle of a field in a valley of wavy corn that made us all smile. None of us had ever seen anything like it before - a huge expanse of golden corn swaying in the breeze either side of the path. Sam pushed on across the bumpy trail through the golden field until we came to a little rise at the far side. He pushed us up to the top from where we could see a gap in a hedge below. The other side of the gap, down the slope, was a gate; a gate to a bungalow - the very same tall wooden gate that stood at the back of Nan's garden. We'd made it to Nan's!

"So what does he think he's going to do now then?"

"There's no way through…we're going to have go all the way back - it will take forever."

"And this time he's bound to get into trouble - you can't just ride across roads like he did earlier, you know."

"Waste of time, waste of time."

"Nan! Nan! - it's me, Sam." There was no answer from the other side of the gate. Sam ran down the slope and started to peer through the small gaps in the fencing. "Over here, Nan, I'm over here!"

"Stuck in a field, stuck in a field, waste of time, waste of time."

"Shut up you two. There's no point stating the obvious - come on what are we going to do?" I thought for a bit. The gate looked quite fragile….if we could just…

"OK everyone - let's charge the gate!"

"What?"

"Let's roll down the hill and smash through the gate - it doesn't look very strong to me."

"Oh great - remember who's here at the front - it's me that going to get it!"

"Come on, come on - let's do it, let's do it - we'll follow, we'll follow." Did the rear wheels have a choice?

Before we knew it, we'd started to roll down the slope. Silently, we gathered speed down the smooth path between the tufts of grass, and front wheel dutifully aimed for the middle of the gate. Being such a heavy old beast meant that we easily smashed through the flimsy wooden panels of Nan's gate and ended up on our side in the middle of the soft green lawn. Sam stood and watched with his mouth agape before realising what it all meant.

"Nan, Nan - it's me!" Sam scrambled through the gaping hole we'd made and ran up the garden path to a bemused Nan who was sat in her conservatory reading the Sunday paper.

The Black Train

On the 2nd Sunday of July 2016 at the mountain resort town of Morzine in the French Alps I witnessed an event that could only be described as a miracle. A small band of men bound only by their loyalty to each other and their adherence to the cycling code, planned and executed the perfect bike race. Despite having an average age of 36 years, an average waist of 36 inches and a combined cycling experience of only 36 months, they contrived to 'win' the 2016 Etape du Tour. For those not in the know about this new cycling Everest, the Etape is designed to give 15,000 road cyclists a chance every year to ride one of the gruelling mountain stages of that years Tour de France. The event comprises a couple of hundred kilometres (all road riding is measured in kilometres because it has a continental European heritage and it sounds a longer distance than if you express it in miles) of torturous mountain climbs ridden non stop a week or so before the professionals complete the same route - albeit at a decidedly faster speed.

Now, if this tale of an extraordinary feat by mere middle-aged men in lycra sounds to be no more than the muddled ramblings of an ageing race bike, then please, bear with me. I was there; I saw it. It was me that was appointed to report the events of that day.

The team, as they were to become, met one evening accidentally. Dan, an estate agent, had recently moved to London from Bristol went to a bar in the City to meet a client. After accidentally bumping into James Hosta who was nursing a bruised shoulder from a recent bicycle accident, he then knocked a jacket belonging to Joe Port - who was with James - onto the floor. Whilst politely apologising for his clumsiness, he couldn't help but get caught staring at a low cut blouse waiting at the bar - being worn by a girl from the office of Ray Amis - who, yes, was also with James and Joe.

"Mate!" Joe was from Sydney, "You oughta look where you're going and not go where you're looking." After more sincere apologising from Dan, the three gradually realised that he was actually quite a good bloke. More importantly, he rode a bicycle and, by the sound of it, followed a similar code to them; He only wore Rapha cycle clothing and his bike was Black. It was good start. Thankfully his client never showed up.

Less than two years later the four of them and us four bikes arrived in Morzine on the Friday before the Etape. The four of them had booked a room each in the most expensive accommodation in town, Le Mas de Couttetaz, and arrived in two large black Mercedes estate cars with enough equipment to run a whole Tour de France team. Dan Grant, my rider, travelled with James, and Joe and Ray were together in the other car. We bikes were properly positioned on the roof in specially made Tour-type roof bars. Everything was right; the tyre decals lined up with the cap-less valves; bar tape, saddles, tyres, everything was black; even the rear quick releases were perfectly positioned at the angle that bisected the seat and chain stays. All that was missing was a sponsors logo on the car door.

Dan was the youngest and fittest member of the team and it had been decided that he would be the finisher. The first three mountain climbs were to be led by his team members - the boys in Black; Rapha-clad, scientifically fuelled and expensively trained for nothing else but to bury themselves for the team; they were to perform the duties of the domestiques. The final points of the plan were laid down late that Friday evening in the hotel bar.

The Saturday morning ride had no more purpose than to shake off the drive from London and make sure that we bikes had survived the trip intact. The serious training had all been completed in the months before; the coach and the nutritionist who'd been employed to ensure that the demanding training plan was adhered to and that they reached the event in perfect condition, were now gone. It was down to us to execute the plan. We, the bikes, were ready for anything but, to be honest, and despite what our riders were saying, we weren't expecting anything really special. These guys were pretty good by the time of the race but their talk was bigger than their legs and even with the impressive weight losses, their bellies still softer than their saddles. They might have done plenty of trips to the Alps to test their climbing and work on their plan but they weren't really competitors - well so we thought.

Just so you know, we bikes were all top of the range road bikes; our riders hadn't skimped on anything - they could afford it. I'm a Trek Madone 9.9 - Dan the Estate Agency owner calls me 'Mad One'; James, the off-shore tax specialist who treats Dan like a son, is the oldest of the group and the only one with any riding experience, rode a Pinarello Dogma (like the one ridden by the Sky team); Joe Port, the wise-cracking Aussie bank trader (known to the others as 'Ritchie' - after the famous Aussie Tour rider Ritchie Porte) rode a blingy Cannondale; quiet and thoughtful Ray Amis rode the unmarked German Bike with the electronic everything - the other three of us bikes thought that he'd got a motor hidden away somewhere in his down-tube but if he had, he wasn't letting on any more than Ray was. Ray was an accountant so he was used to hiding things.

The four of us were all black and the four of them rode only in black Rapha kit. We were quite a sight.

I don't know exactly what happened on the Saturday evening before the race because me and the other bikes were safely tucked up in our rooms. All I do know is that Dan came back around midnight with a pretty American girl and they played around a bit before going back to the bar downstairs with the others. Ritchie's Cannondale told me that something similar happened in his room although he couldn't see exactly what, but they were all in bed by 2am - which was pretty good for them when they were away together. They were clearly focusing on the race.

So what happened? How did they manage to get Dan to be first past the post at the finish in Morzine? Well, they had a plan. Intelligent men, they executed the plan with the ruthless professionalism that only exists in men of their calibre. The plan, combined with a little luck - winners always make their luck - an attention to detail bordering on obsessional (it wasn't just their guns they shaved!), and a combative team spirit put them in the position they needed to be for the second half of the race when the field thinned out. If the team 'spirit' meant bullying their way past slower riders in the early kilometres with angry shouts and judicious shoves when necessary, then so be it; the black train steamed through. Little Dan was the natural climber who'd learned over the months beforehand to conserve his energy over the early climbs whilst the others led the train. They motored up the first climb, Aravis, with Ray leading the way before passing the baton to 'Ritchie' for the Colombine - I'm guessing the German battery was running low on juice by then. James manfully hauled them up the third climb, Ranaz, before descending like a pro for the final climb of the day. By then, the three of them were spent and Dan was left to crest the Joux Plane alone and burst over the finish line in Morzine in front of the cheering crowds. It was all about the bikes; it was all about the preparation. The money men triumphed.

Well, that was how it was supposed to happen. The truth is that the awesome foursome overslept. None of them thought to organise an early morning call - where was Siri when you needed her? By the time James woke the others, around ten, the leading riders, who'd left at 5am to get to the start in Megeve, were half way through the stage. Sneaky Ray suggested that they could still be seen as winners if they were able to sneak onto the course for the last few k's to the finish line, but the others decided against it. Besides, no one would know that they hadn't even started the ride because no one apart from the other competitors actually cares who finishes in the Etape.

Love in Waiting

Two Bromptons, similarly undignified, sat folded on Platform 2 - strike-bound victims making friends as their respective owners made civil conversation in the warmth of the waiting room.

"Where are we?"

"Three Bridges, I think."

"Oh - still a way to go then. He's not happy with all this disruption."

"He looks happy enough to me." I glanced up to see him talking animatedly to the pretty owner of the Red Brompton I was sat with. For those that don't know, we Bromptons are very special bicycles that can be folded up and taken on trains - we're famous for it.

"Hmm...I haven't seen him so happy on a commute for years. What does she do?"

"A yoga teacher. Him?"

"Lawyer - married."

"Really? I always think educated men are so impressive. Is marriage an occupation?"

"No, but it's what he always says."

"Do you think he's told her that? He doesn't look as if he's being 'married' to me." I looked up again and although we couldn't hear what they were saying through the partially steamed windows, he was clearly enjoying talking to her. It had been an hour now. The train indicator boards were still showing nothing due. On a previous occasion he had called the wife to pick him up, but she was out that evening. "No, I think they're discussing more than the weather or how they'll get home. I know that look on her face."

"Do you think they could be falling in love?"

"No, it usually takes longer than an hour."

"But you said you know that look on her face - what did you mean?"

"Well, it's just how I've seen her look before when she's with someone she fancies. She seems to look at them differently. See, her head is slightly bowed and she is having to open her eyes wider to look at him - and now they are changing their positions - see, she has just moved her shoulder back and has pushed her hair away from her face." I was staring at what was going on. The Red Brompton was right - he was definitely fascinated by the yoga teacher. Were they a pair of rail-cross'd lovers changing their lives in front of our eyes?

"I think they're coming out!"

"Here let me have a look." He knelt down with the Red Brompton and deftly felt for movement in her head bearings - I'd had that problem once before so I knew what he was doing.

"His hands are very warm - he sounds ever so nice." Whispering, Red was blushing even redder under his touch. "It feels like he know what he's doing."

"Yes, he does - he's good with Bromptons. He's always tinkering with me." The Yoga teacher stood and watched intently.

"Yes," he said, "there's a little bit of movement - it's easy to fix - I can do it now if you wish?" Within ten seconds he'd expertly untangled Red and stood her on her rear frame. Then, kneeling down again with his Allen keys, he swiftly adjusted the bearings. The yoga teacher rested her hand fondly on the saddle as he did so. When he'd finished, he folded Red away and the two of them returned to the waiting room again. As he held the door open for her to usher her into the warmth, she paused briefly and mouthed 'thank you' to him. Their faces were very close.

Today started like most; the 6.28 from Burgess Hill to East Croydon - a quick change to the London Bridge train and then the short ride to the office in Chancery Lane. The week had been busy and the union strike was starting tomorrow - he'd already decided not to try to get to the office then. The journey home, however, had been foreshortened when the driver stopped at Three Bridges where the train terminated. Most of the other commuters had slowly drifted away and, by 8pm, only the two of them were still holed up in the waiting room. What did they think they were waiting for? There clearly weren't going to be any more trains that night; even the tannoy had been turned off.

"Where were you headed this evening, Red?"

"We live in Haywards Heath - we're coming from a class she takes in East Croydon every Thursday."

"So home is only about ten miles away - she could ride there - you've got lights."

"She doesn't like riding in the dark - and anyway, wouldn't a cab would be a better idea?"

"Yes, but only when or if one or both of them decides that they need to get going. It's not getting any warmer out here!"

We eventually left Three Bridges station at around ten o'clock in a cab headed for Haywards Heath - the two of us were bundled unceremoniously into the boot but we could hear the two of them murmuring in the back seat.

"Who'd have thought we could have talked for so long?" He sounded like a guilty school boy.

"It was really nice - thank you for keeping me company." There was a pause.

"I don't think I'll forget that waiting room." There was some movement and then the sound of a nervous kiss. They had fallen in love! I was right. Yes, it did take longer than an hour, but somehow I knew when he first saw her, he'd fallen in love and she'd smiled back because she knew. In the darkness I sensed a little sigh from Red. They didn't talk again until the cab stopped outside her house. He got out too and, after telling the driver to wait, he got Red from the boot and unfolded her again. The two of them stood and smiled awkwardly at each other. After short pause. they moved together and kissed again with Red in between them.

"Wow," the yoga teacher whispered, "I never thought parting was going to be so hard - good night until tomorrow."

"Yes, Caffe Nero on South Road - see you there at 10." They kissed again slowly and she walked across the road to her house.

Bromptons love to break the rules

Their riders never mad nor fools

Compacted bikes for easy carry

Bromptons made lovers of Sally and Harry

The Parish Counsellor

Erwin Rademaker told everyone he was a Dutchman but within a few months of arriving in the village I realised that this, among other things, wasn't true.

It was during the summer of 1915 that I first saw the new curate of our Parish church of St Mary the Virgin, in Essendon, a neat village tucked away in Hertfordshire. Small in stature with a rough cut face at odds with his soft, slightly-accented voice, he moved with purpose and vigour. As he greeted the congregation at the Lych gate that first Sunday morning with his crisp white collar and somewhat contrived airiness, he drew admiring glances from the women - I soon realised from the warm way he clasped their hands that he was courting the attention. I wasn't watching the workings of an anxious to please new clergyman; Erwin knew what he was doing.

As the Vicar's bicycle, I'd spent much of the past six years leant against the trunk of the Yew tree near the gate, so knew plenty about the comings and goings at the church. Despite my humble beginnings in Nottingham, I always liked to think that being so closely associated with the dour Reverend Higham I'd become an important cog in the workings of the village machine. No one knew as much about the people of the village as the vicar and I. Erwin was very different to the vicar.

Essendon is a quiet place. It's always been that way. Before the war the two hundred and fifty souls of the small village perched on the hill only had the surrounding farms and a few big houses for employment; some of the younger people were now working at the new Telephone Exchange in nearby Hertford, but that was about it. As the second decade of the twentieth century sucked the World into the most brutal human conflict of all time, even quiet little Essendon felt the effects as its own young men joined up to march over the precipice in northern France.

The first inkling I had that he was up to no good was just three weeks after his arrival. Erwin was lodging with crotchety old Mrs Blakey at her red brick cottage in West End Lane. At around 10 o'clock one warm summer evening, he arrived unexpectedly at the churchyard. It was past sundown, as he disappeared into the darkness of the church; I recognized his silhouette against the remains of the day still glowing out to the West; the smell of beer as he passed also told me that he'd spent the past few hours in the Rose and Crown public house. Looking furtively about, he unlocked the creaky vestry door and went inside. A few minutes later he was followed through the same door by a woman; regular Eucharist and Evensong devotee, Mrs Davies, whose husband had tragically gone missing in action the previous year in France; close to, but not actually at the battle of Mons - or so I overheard. The two of them weren't inside for long, but I knew from the clandestine nature of their meeting, that she hadn't gone there to ask Erwin for absolution. My suspicions were proved correct when they left separately; Mrs Davies' flowery summer dress was definitely askew.

Shortly after the incident in the vestry, Erwin started using me to ride around the village. The vicar used me rarely so I had hoped Erwin might but, sadly, his cycling was a bit of a disappointment. The vicar and he had made an agreement so we spent many summer evenings comforting the sad young war widows and giving cheery chats to absent soldiers' loved ones. With a lot of the able men away in France, the women were having to work in the fields and seek comfort and succour from the church; little Erwin must have seemed an inspired engagement by the tall, glacial Reverend Higham; his diligence and attentiveness to the parishioners was completely at odds with the vicar's conspicuous indifference.

As winter approached the days got shorter and our visits begun earlier. Erwin even began to extend our range; we rode to the village of Berkhamsted where Erwin had befriended the local doctor; they always met to drink in the Five Horseshoes. We also went in the other direction down the steep West End Hill to a small group of houses on the edge of Hatfield Park where we met with a young man called Toby Warriner.

Toby, one of the Estate workers, always came out to meet us on the street and closed the door behind him. Apart from his mother, who I never saw, I felt there was something else that he was hiding. Seeing him became a more regular event during the harsh cold of the 1915/16 winter. One day, shortly after Christmas, when curate Erwin had taken Toby a bottle of beer, I overheard them talking. Erwin was being very demanding;

"So when? - when will it happen?" I was surprised how his words had become clipped and more accented; he was clearly agitated.

"I don't know sir," Toby was a simple, deferential type who apparently held the clergy in high esteem, "they said that somethin' would happen in late January."

"Who are they, and what is 'something'?"

"The master, sir. He said yesterday morning that that man from the Navy, you know, that man Churchill, has been to see that area in the Park and he'd said it was good for what they wanted."

"What can the Navy be wanting with the Park?"

"I don't know, sir, but he heard 'im mention that the 'landships' was bein' made now somewhere up north of the country." Erwin seemed to think for a moment.

"Oh well, I guess they have a plan for something. Let's just wait and see. I'll be down again next week and you can let me know if you've heard any more. It would be very interesting to see these 'landships' don't you think?" I got the feeling that Erwin was now being a little patronising. He was clearly more interested than he was making out.

"Oh yes, sir. If I find out when they're coming, then I could take you in to see them - well, not official, of course, but we could watch from the trees if you wanted?"

"Good idea Toby. Now, you keep that mother of yours well." He tapped his nose as he said this. I didn't know what he meant by this but I guessed he had something over the young land worker. Perhaps Toby's mother had been one of the late night visitors to the vestry.

Erwin and I left and, as we pedalled back to Essendon, his face was marked with a smug smile. A little later he hummed himself a triumphant tune as we spun along the bumpy lane. Now I'm no musician, but I would say that the marching tune he hummed wasn't Dutch....it was definitely German. He even sung the words of the last line, 'Und lasst uns alte Kameraden sein'. Whoever sung the marching songs of another countries army?

Despite my reservations, and despite that fact that, as a rider, he treated me particularly badly, I did like Erwin. He seemed oblivious to the Parish politics and the demanding Reverend Higham; it was as if he agreed to everything that was said by the 'old parsnip', as one of the parishioners called him. Erwin did whatever he was told because he knew he had another, more important reason for being there; Erwin had a big secret. For while I couldn't work out what it was until, that was, one day in late January of 1916.

It was the day that I finally discovered who Erwin really was. I thought Toby might have guessed too, but he was so taken in by the lively Curate's interested exterior, and the fact he was a man of the cloth, that he had no reason to think he was up to no good. The hurried trip to meet with the doctor the day after a trip to the forest with Toby, made me think that perhaps he, Dr Kemp, might know something as well, but I wasn't sure. At that time, I thought I was the only one that knew. Erwin Rademaker was a spy. I was being ridden around the village of Essendon by a German spy - I was convinced of it! Now look, I've never pretended I was an angel and I've done my fair share of ungodly things; I once deliberately rode into a dog that always barked at the vicar. I also made one of the young farm lads fall off and break his arm - he thought it would be funny to take me home after an evening at the pub; I decided otherwise. Despite this, I never thought that I would end up working with a spy and possibly betraying my country.

So what happened on that day late in January that gave him away? Well, after seeing Toby on a particularly cold evening, Erwin picked me up straight after Morning Prayer the following day, and we headed back down West End Hill. This time it was so cold and the road so covered in frost that he didn't risk riding me down the ice-covered slope. He slipped to his knees three times with me next to him - thankfully I managed to stay upright. He cursed a lot….in German.

We finally arrived outside Toby's house and he came out with his buttoned great coat and a woollen scarf wrapped high around his face. Silently we crossed the field opposite the house and Erwin walked with me between the two of them into the woods. There were no real paths but Toby seemed to know the way through the thick undergrowth. After a while I saw a large clearing with a series of trenches dug across it; the three of us ducked down behind some dense brambles. After an hour or so, a number of heavily overcoated and hatted men came from the direction of the large house - Hatfield House - over to the right, and gathered behind a low rope strung between posts. Then we saw it. To be correct, we heard it first - a huge black, steel, rhomboid-shaped behemoth that rattled its way across the field at walking pace towards the waiting reception committee - I heard later that they were men of very high rank and included that Churchill man, Lord Kitchener himself and even the Prime Minister, Mr Lloyd George. The monster stood over eight feet high and belched the filthy fumes of a combustion engine as it crissed-crossed the trenches and the marshy, barb-wire covered stretches of the clearing.

Erwin was clearly fascinated and stared hard at the exhibition from his crouched position behind the bush. The 'show' ended with shells being fired from gun ports protruding from each side of the beast. The noise was deafening.

"So this is what they are planning." Erwin, breathless, was clearly in raptures.

"Yes, Mr Rademaker, this'll show the Hun what we're made of."

"So will they be ready soon?"

"My friend at the house said he heard one of the Navy men saying that we ought to have 3,000 of them!" I genuinely saw Erwin's eyes widen in wonderment; something that usually only happened to him in the presence of women.

Later that evening we pedaled off to the Five Horseshoes again and, from my resting place outside, I saw Erwin in deep conversation with the doctor through the steamy pub window; he was clearly explaining what he'd seen earlier in the day in the Hatfield grounds - I could tell by the shapes described by his hands that he was talking about the landships.

A few days later, Erwin took me to Hatfield Railway Station and stood with me in the Guards van to Kings Cross Station in London - there he rode me to a small house off York Way and disappeared inside for an hour or so before before taking me home again. We did this trip a few times over the following months and I never knew who he was seeing or why; but it was nice to ride around the busy city roads for a change.

After all this excitement, things died down for a while. Erwin went back to his cold evening rides around the Parish and his occasional assignations in the vestry with the lonely ladies; some of them were even allowed to ride me home after their couplings, which was a rather odd, melancholy, experience. Over time I almost forgot that Erwin was a spy.

When the Spring arrived, the mood in the village began to lighten, people started to meet again in the streets and the children played in the field behind the Church again. There was the wonderful day in March when the late snow fell with heavy flakes for a whole night, and happy families came out to toboggan the slope on all manner of household sleds and boards of wood; most of the winter on top of the hill had just been cold, wet and windy so it was a relief to see everyone smiling again. The growing excitement of those early months of 1916, suggested that we might be seeing an end to the war; but, as had happened in the previous year, the lack of news of heavy conflict was simply because the opposing armies were having to combat the penetrating cold and the foul conditions of their trenches rather than each other. The monumental battle of The Somme that July proved that there was to be no let up, and that the opposing sides were still intent on pummelling each other to a standstill on that fractious Western Front. Word of more village casualties began to filter back and the mood became sombre again.

In the middle of July, something else happened which put Erwin under more pressure and me with a difficult choice. I was already feeling guilty for being party to his spying and irreverent activities, but I didn't know what else I could do. I was being drawn into his world of espionage and subterfuge as an innocent bystander. Then one particularly sunny day I felt that I was given an opportunity that could assist Erwin's cause. Please believe it wasn't that I wanted to help a spy; I just thought that Mrs Davies was being particularly unfair on him. It all started in the churchyard when she apprehended him near the gate as he was leaving to go for his lunch one day.

"Mr Rademaker, sir, have you got a minute." Plump Mrs Davies in a high-necked smock, was as deferential to the clergy as Toby was.

"Yes, Mrs Davies, how can I help?" He sensed, as I did, that this wasn't a social enquiry about booking the vestry for the evening.

"Well, sir, this is a bit difficult but, well, I'm pregnant with our child." I watched him closely; his expression didn't change but I'm sure I saw his jaw set a little as he thought through the implications of being responsible for a child with an enemy war widow - there was also the suggestion however that part of him thought that it might look good on his record as proof of his commitment to the cause.

"Oh." He paused briefly. "So I suppose you will be wondering what you should do - I mean, this could lead to some difficulties for you - your widows pension being withdrawn, for example?" Whilst it was true that some local pensions offices had been reported as doing exactly that to widows who they thought were behaving in the 'wrong' way, it was a harsh thing to say. Mrs Davies' face fell in disappointment but, at the same time, I could see bitterness bristle in her eyes.

"So you're not going to...!" Before she finished Erwin put his hands out to hers and, holding them firmly, he looked into her eyes in the way he always did, and spoke to her in a firm, but reassuringly comforting, tone.

"Please, Mrs Davies, Ethel. The war is making life hard for all of us. I can see that the loss of your husband, Reginald, still weighs heavily on you, so I think we should take some time to think things through properly. But first, I think you should go to see a doctor friend of mine in Little Berkhamsted - just to be sure that everything is, you know, as it should be. I will give you a letter which you should give to him. You can take the bicycle now if you wish?" It wasn't really a question. "Just wait there a moment and I'll write you an introduction." Erwin disappeared into the vestry and Mrs Davies turned and looked slightly scathingly at me. I could tell that she knew I was in cahoots with the curate and I guess she had heard of his jaunts around the village on the Church bike to visit other women who'd lost loved ones. I saw a tear roll down her cheek as the enormity of what might be suggested by the curate and the doctor dawned. I knew that she had now become a threat to him and to our little world in the village. If this got out then he might have to leave and there would be no one to do his good works.

A few minutes later Mrs Davies and I left the village and wobbled down Cucumber Lane towards Little Berkhamsted; Mrs Davies was clearly not an experienced cyclist, and although I was no racing machine - Erwin had kept me nicely oiled and my wheels ran free and true - we were moving along more quickly than I think she anticipated we would. I realised there was an opportunity for me. As we accelerated down the slope I resisted the temptation to allow the pressure she was putting on the brake levers to actually connect to the wheels; consequently our speed began to rise. It went up and up. We were never going to make the left hand bend into Berkhamsted Lane and Mrs Davies should never have attempted it. We didn't even get close and, instead, we ran straight across the junction and into the thick bushes on the opposite side. Ordinarily, they might have cushioned her fall, but the tall Larch tree hidden just behind the broad-leaved hedge did not. Mrs Davies' head struck the trunk at around twenty-two miles an hour and her death was instantaneous.

A week later I observed the funeral with a deliberate detachment from my place against the Yew; Mrs Davies' coffin was carried sedately from the horse drawn hearse towards the clean cut hole in the ground I'd watched being dug by the grubby grave-digger the previous day. It was a nice spot with a clear view - one that she wouldn't appreciate - down the hill to the West. The large congregation - Mrs Davies was a popular village figure - was commendably sombre and the summer breeze in the leaves was interrupted occasionally by the sheepish muffled sniffs of the village women folk. There appeared to be no knowledge of the pregnancy, and the Reverend Higham and Erwin conducted the funeral with the necessary propriety and solemnity. Erwin's face gave nothing away, although I'm sure he glanced over to me at one point; I think he treated me slightly differently from that day on. I actually like to think he might have known that I was entirely responsible for the accident that caused the death of Mrs Davies. Thankfully, his sealed letter she had carried in her purse at the time of her death, was given to the doctor to whom it was addressed and handled, again, with the necessary discretion. Nothing was ever divulged about it contents, but I was sure that Erwin had suggested some sort of termination of the pregnancy to the doctor. The night before the funeral the two of them had met at the Five Horsehoes for their regular discussion at the quietest table in the corner of the bar.

In August, the summer was at its height with glorious sunny days and warm sticky nights, but Erwin was definitely feeling the strain; he was waiting for something. Our weekly visits to see Toby were getting more anxious. Every time they met, Erwin got more forceful. I once saw him push Toby up against the side of the house and grasp him by his collar. It seemed odd that a slight man of the cloth should be able to exert such a physical imposition over the stoutly built estate worker, but Erwin's demeanour was as rugged as his face, and at times like this he acquitted his undercover calling. When he was after information he knew how to extort it from people.

Finally, at the the end of August he seemed to get what he was looking for. It was one of our weekly visits to see Toby and the young man was, unusually, waiting outside for us by the side of the road. He seemed excited and clearly had something for Erwin.

"Sir", he exclaimed before we'd even come to halt, "Sir, I think I have it." Erwin wasn't going to be rushed - he'd heard promises like this before. He carefully put me against the wall of the house and turned toward Toby.

"Hello Toby - what exactly do you think you have?"

"This sir!" He held up a small sheaf of papers which looked to have drawings and numbers on them. Erwin took them and examined them carefully. I could just make out the familiar rhomboid shapes.

"Hmm, I'm not sure - where are they from?" He looked sternly at Toby.

"Oh, one of the butlers saw them on his Lordship's desk and took them."

"He did what?"

"Well, not all of them, just some of them."

"And his Lordship didn't notice?"

"No - the butler said that his lordship doesn't read much of the paperwork he brings home - I don't think he understands it to be honest." Erwin look at him with slight admonishment - it really wasn't for Toby to question his employers intelligence.

"Well, as you know, I have wanted to see these plans for a while - my friends in the Army have been intrigued to know what the Navy have been up to." I knew this was a lie - but it contained an element of truth; the 'Army' that Erwin was referring to was almost certainly the Imperial German Army and not, as I assumed Toby thought, the British Army.

Things happened quite quickly after this. We flew back up the hill to the village with the papers tucked away in his pocket and, panting, he left me outside Mrs Blakey's house and disappeared inside. After a few minutes there was a brief commotion with raised voices - well, Mrs Blakey raised her voice. As quickly as it had started, it suddenly went quiet and he came out again. Something had happened which wasn't very good. Erwin was in a panic; he grabbed me and, stomping on my pedals and muttering away in German, he rode me furiously out of the village, past the water tower, and down the hill towards Little Berkhamsted - it could only be the Doctor that we were going to see. I was right, but instead of meeting the doctor in the public house as usual, Erwin rode me to a big house further down the road. Throwing me against the hedge outside, he marched into the garden and thumped loudly on the door.

The doctor eventually came out and calmed him down - I couldn't hear everything that was being said but Doctor Kemp's voice did sound to be soothing Erwin. They were still inside the garden, behind the hedge, but as Erwin was about to leave I heard a few bits and pieces of their conversation.

"I think she's dead…."

"…as I said, Erwin, don't worry - I will sort it out." A minute later, "..you wait and see tonight - there will be a lot of Zeppelins - just stay at the church and Mrs Blakey will be all sorted by the morning." Finally I heard one slightly plaintive snippet from Erwin,

"So these will get to the right people?" Erwin could only have been talking about the plans with the landship drawings.

I had not the slightest idea what the Doctor had been talking about but I got the feeling that he was saying that he would sort out whatever had happened back at Mrs Blakey's house.

Erwin rode me back to Essendon very slowly. Stopping at the first house in the village just after the Water Tower - where Mrs Bullard lived alone as her husband, Brigadier Thomas 'Bully' Bullard, was away in France - Erwin went inside. I decided that the 'visits' to the wives waiting for news of their husbands away at war was as much for him to glean information about proposed military plans written in letters from the Front, as much as it was him getting his leg over. But this time, I think he just wanted somewhere to be other than at his lodgings. I think that Mrs Blakey must have discovered something…perhaps Erwin had the left the plans on the table and she'd found them!

We didn't leave the Bullard's until around 10pm, and after stopping off at the Rose and Crown we went to the Church. I was left in my usual place against the yew tree and Erwin disappeared into the darkened vestry once more. Nothing happened for some time. The sun finally set in the west and the sky slowly turned to an inky black. The village was dark and the air was still.

After a couple of hours, I became aware of a noise. It was only a very low hum but there was definitely a noise coming from the north. Imperceptibly, the sound grew louder. It was then interrupted by another, much closer sound, that I recognised. Erwin had opened the still creaky vestry door and was coming down the steps. He walked slowly to the edge of the churchyard and gazed out into the night in the direction of the noise. Then I saw them. Thirteen huge cigar shaped objects floating in the sky. They were at least three miles away over Hatfield and travelling slowly south in the direction of London. I had heard the word 'Zeppelin' from a couple of half-caught conversations in the village, and I had always assumed that they were some sort of German gun or aeroplane that had been attacking London. So this is what the Doctor was talking about. I had never seen or heard anything like these huge eerie objects advancing across the dark skies under the half light of the moon. Erwin stood with an almost reverential pose and seemed to rise up at the power of the vision in front of him. His country was bringing a heavenly destruction upon the people of London.

Forty minutes later - Erwin was still stood watching, even though there wasn't much to be seen any more - except for a sudden bright yellow flash in the sky to the south. I later learned that one of the German airships had been shot down near Cuffley by an intrepid English pilot from the Royal Flying Corps. As the glow of the fireball died down, I became aware of the sound of the Zeppelins, well one of them at least, coming in our direction - it was much closer to us this time and coming straight for us. Closer and closer it got, until I could see very little else in the sky. Erwin raised his arms as if to hail the flying leviathan - he began to jump up and down with joy. The sound of the engines was deafening. Then, just as it seemed that it would strike the tower of the church, the nose began to rise and it soared up over us. At the same moment, a whistling sound could be heard; whistling, followed by a dull thud and then a huge explosion in the field behind the church. The Zeppelin was dropping its bombs on Essendon. Erwin stood still before turning and running back towards me with a look of fear. The last I saw of him was when he barged through the vestry door and slammed it behind him. A second later the vestry itself exploded in a huge ball of flame and dust as a bomb smashed through the roof and detonated inside.

After a few minutes, futile screams could be heard from the village. A number of bombs had hit and destroyed houses and two young girls were tragically killed at the forge. There was no panic; instead, a very English response to the disaster ensued. The village bobby, his uniform still undone, was on the scene within minutes and everyone was returned to their homes with calmness. Apart from the two girls, no one else was injured and the majority of the bombs fell on open ground surrounding the village; the damage was much less than it could have been.

I stood there, unnoticed, against the Yew with the wreckage of the vestry strewn about in front of me. Huge lumps of stone lay across the path and the inside of the church could be seen through the gaping hole left by the explosion. At first light, the Bobby returned with another man in a trench coat with a very official bearing. It took me a while to realise that it was the Doctor. The two of them searched the rubble for a few minutes before finding what was obviously the remains of Erwin buried underneath. Nothing was said. The area was cordoned off and later that morning, after Lord Cecil arrived from Hatfield House to show official support for the villagers, some other men came and, before anyone else knew about it, brought out Erwin's body and took it away. When Lord Cecil arrived it was the Doctor that had met him and gave him a large brown envelope - he looked like he knew him - before conducting the tour of the damage. I never saw or heard anything about it again. It transpired that Mrs Blakey's house was also destroyed in the bombing and her body found inside; another unfortunate victim of German aggression on mainland England - albeit at the hands of Erwin and not the Zeppelin.

It was a long time before I was ever looked at again - both my tyres had been punctured by shrapnel from the explosion and there was a big dent in my crossbar from a piece of falling masonry that had put me all out of shape and probably useless. A short while later I was moved away and put in a storage building at the back of the pub. I'm still here. I don't regret my part in the deaths of those two ladies, and I'll never forget being ridden around the village by Erwin. He was a bad man, but a charmer; he was a spy, but he also kept the home fires burning.

[The first tanks were deployed by the French Army in April 1917 at the Nivell Offensive and later that year on September 15th the British Mk 1 tanks were used at the Battle of Flers-Courcelette (part of the Battle of the Somme). The Germans never knew about the development of the tank in Britain - by the end of the war, the British and French had produced many thousands of tanks between them whereas the Germans had managed only 20.]

Taken for a Ride

I might look like a tired old replica of Bernard Hinault's 1985 Tour de France winning bike, but there is more to me than meets the eye.

I realised I had to say something last Thursday when a strangely familiar man, gaunt for his years, walked into my shop in Gravesend where I've been hung all these years and asked for Paul. He didn't seem like a cyclist - more like a tax inspector. Even young Toby sensed that the man wanted something more pressing than a puncture repair and shouted down to the boss in the basement.

"Yes, sir, what can I do to..." Breathing heavily from hauling his paunch up the stairs and having barely looked up before speaking, Paul's voice tailed away quickly when he saw the man in the raincoat in his shop. "Mickey? What do you want?" A flick of his head signalled Toby to leave them.

"I've come for the bike. Bernie wants his bike back." Mean eyes glanced in my direction as Mickey paused. "He don't want the money no more either." Paul also glanced up at me briefly; he looked haunted, like he'd seen a ghost.

"Why does he want it back?"

"He just does - that's it. I'll come with a van next week."

And that was it. Now, I knew I wasn't the only replica that came from Bernie's workshop because a few of us had been made at the same time and some of the customers had mentioned they'd seen frames like me in other shops in Kent, but I never thought we'd actually be going back after all these years.

You see, it all started in the Spring of 1984 when a man called Kenny went to Bernie's place on Brocket Lane in Hainault. Bernie had been a bike frame builder for years and had a big house and garden that backed onto the forested grounds of Alder house. He rented a workshop in Stratford where the lads assembled his bikes, but he preferred to work alone in the shed at the end of his garden. Carmel and the kids knew to keep away from him there and only his young boy, Mickey, ever took any interest in what his Dad got up to.

The result of that meeting with Kenny was a delivery late the following evening. A Transit reversed up the side of the house and the driver and Bernie hauled the contents to the back of the shed and covered it up with tarpaulin. I never saw Kenny again or the Transit. Me and the others were made from that pile of metal. It took Bernie the best part of a year and a half, but by the end he had produced eighteen beautiful replicas of Bernard Hinault's winning bike - the one he won the '85 Tour with. Spraying us all with silver paint like Hinault's made him chuckle. We were then mounted on wall boards and clearly marked as for 'Display Only' - he further ensured we would never be ridden by making the bottom bracket tube from a solid billeted piece of metal.

Now, making replica bike frames may not sound like such an odd thing for a frame builder to do, but you have to be aware that the material that he was working with wasn't his usual stuff. We replicas weren't made from common or garden Reynolds 531 or even the revered 753 steel with the double butted tubes; we weren't made from the nasty aluminium stuff that was popular at the time; we certainly weren't made like them monocoque carbon-fibre frames that everyone rides nowadays and which is regarded as the best material ever invented. No, we was made from something far more valuable; something that has been worshipped for thousands of years as the most beautiful metal ever pulled from the ground; the Egyptians buried their pharaohs with us and the great nations of the world hid us away in huge vaults as a mark of their countries' value. We are gold. We were made from solid bricks of stolen gold that Bernie melted down in the back of his shed and formed into lengths of tubing. He cut lugs from thin sheets of the same gold bricks to hold us together and then, during the hot August of 1985 , he carefully soldered us into the most beautiful frames - before hastily daubing us with dull grey-blue primer. Once this was applied we were no longer hidden away in the back of the shed; we were then hung in the windows where we could watch his kids play rough in the garden and Carmel by the pool in her bikini.

After we was finished we hung around for a few weeks and the remaining bricks at the back of the shed under the tarpaulin slowly disappeared. There were about 120 bricks in all and we each took a brick to make….so we was heavy for a bike frame. Everything was done by Bernie on his own; most evenings he'd slip a couple of bricks in his rucksack just before he took the two dobermans, Jonny and Matt for a walk in the forest out the back. After their walk he'd wash his hands in the shed before going indoors for tea with Carmel and the kids. Bernie was a creature of good habits.

At the time it didn't occur to me that Bernie's house was that big, but years later, a few months before Mickey turned up, I overheard a muffled conversation about him in the shop between Paul and another man who'd said he was a policeman but neither looked nor sounded like one.

"Alright Paul - how's things?" He sounded more Essex than Kent.

"Good, good - shouldn't moan."

"Seen Bernie recently?"

"Nah - not for a quite a few years."

"Oh - I saw him down the lodge the other week - seems to be keeping well - not bad for 79. Life done him OK I think."

"Yeah - after the start he had you wouldn't have thought it possible."

"What, you mean when he was a lad with Kenny and they was sent to borstal - they was a right handful those two - you know they was done for stealing bikes?"

"Yeah - and then he ended up making them! Who'd have thought it."

"Well, that's what it looked like - but most of his dosh came from other jobs, you know that?" Paul smirked.

"Yeah, I know." There was tinge of regret in his voice; perhaps he wished he'd gone that way too. The bike shop he took over in the late seventies from his father gave him a good living but he'd never been a rich man. Not like Kenny or Bernie.

Not long after the '85 Tour, a man called Rob came to see us hanging up in Bernie's shed.

"So what do you want me to do with these then Bernie?" Rob was a rep from the bike trade who had sold Bernie's frames to shops in the past.

"Well, I want you to give them to shops, you know - as sort of adverts for my skills. I want them hung in all the best bike shops in Essex and Kent. Oh yes, and I want them to pay for them too. They're going to pay me every month just to have them." Robert looked in amazement at Bernie before looking a little more closely at me, in particular, as if looking for a faults in Bernie's work. There weren't any.

"Why would they pay for them Bernie?" He didn't seem to understand; perhaps he didn't know Bernie very well. There was a pause as Bernie collected himself.

"Cos you're going to tell them that I said they have to - and you're going to get a cut of the money." Rob seemed to fail to detect the menace in the words. "Listen, Robert, come here. I know you're young and quite new at this, but I guarantee that when you go and see them, they'll willingly take them OK? Know what I mean?" I'm not sure that Robert did, but he nodded all the same.

"What do I tell the boss?"

"You don't tell him anything!" After his mauling, Rob left us. Then, one by one over the next few weeks, we were picked up by him and taken away to a shop. I was the last to leave.

I don't know what will happen next - I guess we'll be melted down and put back into bricks. Then we'll probably end up in another vault again. I've liked being in the shop and people looking at me over the years, but I wish I could have been a proper bike. I have felt a bit of a fraud.

Out The Back Door

I always know when it's happened. I don't have any strange sixth; there are just a couple of signs that tell me that all is not right. I feel it first when the back door latch clicks - there's a small hesitation of the sound as the door opens because he's resting on the handle. If it's a particularly still morning I can hear him moving gingerly around the kitchen before coming outside. In those first few moments my suspicions are roused. On such days, when he finally emerges from the house I just have to see his face to know that I'm right.

Every weekend morning as the sun starts to colour the garden, I wait in chilled anticipation for our ride - I never know where we're going and I don't know who we're going to meet - but after five days locked in the shed I just can't wait to get out. Every Saturday and Sunday we go out to the hills and, for the sheer pleasure of it, we ride. Without fail our rides always takes longer than he thinks they will and his lunch is always cold. But she doesn't seem to mind too much.

We've been together for three years now and I think I'm here to stay - his previous bike didn't last very long. He's looked after me well and kept me properly serviced to the point where I don't think that he'll be getting another bike; we even have two sets of wheels - one set for the winter and another lighter, more expensive set for the summer.

By the time he has lifted a leaden foot over the back door step I'm beginning to brace myself for the long wincing walk down the garden path that follows on days like these. In case you hadn't realised, Glenn suffers from a chronic back problem - 'low grade isthmic spondylolisthesis' as he once described it to another cyclist. The result is two herniated discs which occasionally flare up and cause him intense pain. The suffering he endures from simply walking down the garden path would send anyone else back to bed crying to their God for forgiveness for whatever it was that they had done so wrong. It looks like a wretched ex-lover, needle in hand, is stabbing at the spine of a lycra-clad doll.

But Glenn never turns back. Tall, fit, lean Glenn continues his miserable hobble to the garden shed and, after spending a full ten minutes painfully unlocking me from my prison, he pushes me to the rear gate and then out to the road - I feel his hands shaking at every twinge. Eventually I'll be sat next to the kerb and he'll go through his preparation to climb on.

The first time this happened I feared the worst. I was convinced that at this point we would collapse to a painful heap at the side of the road and we'd lay there twisted and incapacitated until the milkman or an inquisitive dog walker found us. That first time it seemed to take an age for him to pluck up the courage to attempt to ride me - but I think he knew something; something that no doctor, back specialist or smart-alec sports physio would even suggest was possible for someone in his condition. Most of them know little about the realities of back pain; the sleepless nights, the debilitating side-effects of their useless painkillers, the contorted body shapes. They only ever see a patient when he or she is free enough of pain to 'present' themselves at the surgery....that band of highly-paid National Health professionals who care little for an apparently fit bicycle riding patient, who is unlikely to die of their complaint (yes, they seem to consider that back pain sufferers are complainers), and whose outward appearance is fine. There is almost the hint that back sufferers who cycle are, in some way, responsible for their problems. Glenn doesn't like doctors any more than he likes the burning pain. No, Glenn has worked out that riding a bicycle is the best prescription when things get bad and that he would be rewarded for the exertions required to reach this point at the back of the garden.

Patiently waiting, I'm well aware that getting started is the most painful part; it takes all of Glenn's will to lift his leg around the saddle so that he can stand astride me, his hands gripping my bars as if his life depended on it. I can sense the coruscating tension of those erector spinae muscles in spasm as they grip his lower back with the intensity of a fighter's fist and shoot pulsing pains down the sciatic nerve into the core of his right calf. Bravely, he lifts his left foot and cleats it to the pedal as if trying not to let his back know what we are about to do, and then, with a sharp intake of breath and another wince of pain, he pushes us away.

The first few seconds are equally intense as he raises his backside to the saddle and slides it back. Then follows another brief moment of concern as he clicks his right foot into the other pedal. Success! We are off.

With the slow increase in speed, I feel those same lower back muscles start to relax; their job of supporting his arms head and torso over his pelvis is done for now. Hands and pelvis take the strain away from his back which is now suspended between the two; even the pain in his leg subsides. More pressure on the pedals only increases the relief; the road is now ours and Glenn is beginning to smile. We'll try not to stop until we return home because dismounting and walking is so painful - until that time, we will climb the twisty hills and speed down the valleys walls without so much as a tweak from his back.

However much it hurts me to see Glenn in so much pain on these early mornings, the struggle out of the back door is worth it.

Stage Revolution

Being bicycles, we're more than familiar with revolutions; our wheels complete them every time we move. We've even been known to stage the sort of revolutions that result in us overthrowing riders when things aren't going well - yes we can crash when we want to, you know. However, being so discontented that we wanted to change the way the sport of cycle racing is governed was never discussed - until last years Tour de France, that is.

"No no no, that's enough! He just put that bike over the edge!" The dismay in his words was clear; we'd heard cries like this too often over the past week or so. Riders were taking it out on bikes when it was they that were under-performing; the bike in this incident, Astana 4, had been crashed when the young rider misjudged a sharp bend on the previous descent and slid painfully on lycra'd buttocks along the stony apron. Standing bloodied over the machine, he'd viciously stamped through the carbon crossbar before throwing the mangled wreck into the abyss. Never before had there been a Grand Tour with so many incidents like this. Of course, none of the TV viewers would have seen or heard what was said; it wasn't good for the sport to see disgruntled riders blaming their bikes. Besides, the sponsors wouldn't like it either.

"Come on guys, we all know what the prima donna riders are like. Hey, Bianchi 7, just be thankful you don't have that monster German rider on Giant 3 grinding your pedals and bending your bars at the slightest incline - and Movistar 1? you really are the lucky one; your little fella can't weigh more than a bag of Colombian coffee!"

"I don't know why you're so cheerful, Scott." Ridley 9, who we called Arnold on account of his old kit and even older rider, had been ridden in the previous years Tour and was at the end of his tether. Usually, us Tour bikes get sold off to the highest bidder at the end of the race - usually to some fat middle-aged millionaire with more airmiles and lunches under his belt than cycle miles. But poor old Arnold was only ever going to get a middling, bottle-carrying 'domestique' for this Tour (a rider with no chance of winning anything other than a share in his team leaders winnings), and, because his team was so badly funded, he was called back for another year of servitude. "This rider of mine only seems happy when he is moaning about me - I wish he'd put some work into the pedals!" Giant 3, with the muscular German sprinter on board, was suffering a lot of pain so had to say something.

"Be careful what you wish for." Despite being from a Taiwanese company, Giant 3 had a decidedly Dutch outlook on account of having been assembled in their Netherlands factory. "I heard that last years bike ridden by the bully sat on me now, ended up being bought by the Chief of a German bank with no intention of riding; it now hangs on a Boardroom wall in Frankfurt with a stressed-out steerer and a monocoque in crisis; what makes those people do that? That's not how you want to go, is it?"

The truth is that, whatever the Press and the team managers tell you, there really isn't much between us bikes anymore - we all work hard every day to deliver the results for our riders and they either get the glory when they win or the blame when they don't. Some of them bully us and treat us badly, but most are completely ambivalent - we're just bikes. And, till now, we've just got on with the job.

Go back forty years and it was very different. The riders back then used to love their bikes and they all had their favourite frame builders - some bikes were decidedly better than others. Nowadays, though, we're basically the same. This might make it seem fairer for the people that follow the sport and who think that riders are the only arbiter of success or failure, but it makes the claims of the manufacturers, who put their names on our identikit-carbon frames, sound a bit hollow - in the glory days some of the riders even had their favourite frame sprayed up with the name of their team sponsors! When Lance Armstrong said 'it's not about the bike' he was wrong (I think he was referring to something other than his own talent for why he won so easily!) - but try and tell the riders of today that we're the same; our diminutive divas are convinced that the other teams have illegal bikes that make them go faster. Apart from the bikes with the hidden electric motors (all the teams have got them, you know - they are given to the weakest riders in the team time trial or the superstars that just fancy a day off) we're all made of the same stuff and many of us are even from the same factory. We all still have a soul, and it comes from the heart of our designers; be they Italian, French, Spanish. But whilst it's their beat we feel, their spirit we carry along the roads, we're all the same.

So how do the bikes in the peloton feel about the way we're regarded? Well, I think that for years we have just put up with the slow erosion of our importance in the winning of races - the international rule-makers haven't helped with their insistence that, just as with Formula One motor racing, no one is allowed to develop an unfair technical advantage - but the mood in the peloton has been changing. We've been waiting for someone to 'do' something, but they haven't; what happened to ingenuity of the British? - you'd have thought they could have come up with something a bit better than 'marginal gains'. It seems that 'staying within the rules' has dented any spark of progress with us bicycles - rim brakes? Derailleurs? - weren't all these invented over half a century ago? I suppose we have always stupidly believed that the law makers of the sport and the riders have had our best intentions at heart - the bike is the star, they say; their sport is about the greatest invention known to man. Their insistence on refusing to allow technical progress whilst, at the same time, and most incredibly, expanding the greatest show on earth to include more and more European nations for the route, has been the last straw. Nothing has diluted the respected traditions of the spectacle more than this - the Tour de France in Yorkshire? What were they thinking? Everyone knows that the British riders are only really good at the time trials because for years that was all they were allowed to do in their car-infested country; or is it just about selling more of their bikes to the island mamils? There aren't even any mountains there. 'La Tour' is La France, and it should stay here. At this rate they'll be merging it with the Giro d'Iltalia and the Vuelta a Espana into some great European stage race series.

Things need to change. I've heard the rumblings. Some of the smaller team bikes have been colluding with the big boys to throw some of the stages - the bikes are going to even things up a bit; we're going to start promoting those bikes that have real heritage - the ones that don't get a chance to race at the finish. We're going to split the sport from within.

"How many climbs is it today?" Despite his name, Focus 2 never knew what was going on.

"Two category 1's, one category 2, a couple of category 3's and one Hors Categorie."

"So how many climbs is that?"

"6!" Giant 3 was losing patience and groaning heavily under the onslaught of the frame-flexing power of his riders' massive legs. "You might like to think you're from Germany, but your inattention to detail proves you're no more than a Far Eastern import like the rest of us."

"Hey!" All the Bianchi's still think they are made in Italy like they always used to be - and Bianchi 7 wasn't going to have his heritage besmirched. "Bianchi e molto speciale di biciclette!" Not even Giant 3 wanted to upset a Bianchi because they'd been around for so long and, well, there was something quaint about their old-school Italian ways. So why not only allow bikes made by their sponsor countries be allowed to participate? It's not as if making a carbon frame is hard - just decide that the brand has to be designed and built in its own country.

"Yes, sorry Edoardo. Guys, look, I'm sorry but I don't think I'm going to able to finish today; my bottom bracket is doomed. I'm going to have to give out at the bottom of the next climb."

"That's a really good idea Giant - I might ask to be excused as well. I'm too old and tired for this." Arnold sidled over to the side of the peloton and prayed to God to be free of his thankless rider. The mood everywhere was quite low.

"Any more of you lot want to leave this race?" I thought I would test the metal of the peloton's feelings - not that there is much metal in a peloton these days. "Who else is fed up with listening to all those team 'Presidents' buying bad blood with backers money to win races? Anyone else dislike the faceless regulators with their nit-picking directives on how we're constructed?"

"Yeah, permission to speak, sir - you can count us boys in too!" Now, I really didn't expect the Trek bikes to join in, but, it was true that they were suffering a similar lack of identity in the US to the rest of us in Europe; even one of the Specialised bikes nodded his approval.

The voices were getting louder. The Peloton was genuinely in revolt.

"So come on Scott, Mr Popular, what do you think should we do?" I didn't really know how to answer the Pinarello.

"We could crash?" The Swiss BMC's never had much imagination.

"Do you think that's wise, sir? It wouldn't change anything - they'll just give the riders new bikes from cheaper factories and we'll be binned." It was quite a perceptive thought from the deferential Pinarello 5 - the one who'd only joined us that day on account of his predecessor suffering from the usual Dogma dilemma - a broken frame; something that our steel forebears never suffered. But the little squabble had given me a moment to think; I had an idea.

"OK, guys, don't panic - how about this? How about we just go slow on the final two climbs. Really slow so that no one can get away. So slow that the riders know something is up but have no idea what. Let's get the TV crews talking about us for once. Lets make the 'powers-that-be' take notice. They need to know that we want to make a difference. This is supposed to be a bike race and we're the bikes!"

"Then," Trek 3 was clearly getting excited, "in tomorrows stage we'll throw a few chains for the leaders and get the domestiques to drop their bottles. This could be fun!"

It was just the start. Our actions in the next few days of the Tour were to change things forever. It wasn't about going back to how things used to be - it was about taking back control of our sport. Making it a race again; making it longer and harder like it used to be - because true glory can only be achieved when a race tests the muscle, character and will of the best riders with the best bikes. Vive la Tour! Vive la bicyclette!

Fixed For Christmas

I've just been through the toughest weeks of my life. It all started when he decided he needed more money for Christmas so took a job in Central London. Now, you might think that this would seem like a sensible idea for a young man in his final year of university who is up to his overdraft limit; until you realise that the job entailed him riding me around the streets of the busy roads of the capital for ten hours a day. Yes, he thought it was a cool to be a cycle courier; he'd learn the streets of London on a bike and get paid for it!

Now in 1984, dispatching was a motorbike-only occupation; turning up for a Monday morning 'interview' in a scruffy office over a shop just off the Kings Road in cycling shorts and cap, and riding a fixed wheel bicycle, didn't go down too well.

"What bike you got mate?" It was the very first question and, I suppose, one he should have expected.

"Er…a bicycle?"

"No mate - what bike you got?"

"I don't have one - I've got a bicycle?" As you might imagine, this wasn't a great start to the interview, but, amazingly, after twenty minutes of polite cajoling with the fat controller who initially decided he was talking to a complete idiot, we managed to clinch a weeks trial - and one where they would only give him the short drops around the City and West End - the jobs the motorcyclists didn't like to do on account that they didn't pay enough. The best thing about this arrangement was that there was no suggestion he should be on a different pay rate to the 'proper' dispatchers; if he was happy to just do the short runs then he could 'ave 'em.

So armed with a state of the art BT pager that would beep out details of jobs, and a brand new A-Z with the coloured (but not waterproof) central pages, we set out on our first pick-up; a brave new world of getting on not just his metaphorical bike when all around were striking their jobs out of existence. To be honest, we didn't know our way around London, and I doubted it would last. But surprisingly he got used to map reading and the first day passed quite quickly. We started in a sun-filled Sloane Square, went up through Knightsbridge to Marble Arch, before being sent to the City for a few lunchtime jobs. Then, after a short break with a pinta milk and a pasty around 2.00 o'clock in a park near Old Street, we were back to the bustling West End. The day ended with a circular trip of BT offices from Holborn to Vauxhall and Chelsea. Easy. Sadly, the sunny start to our new job ended there and then.

Tuesday morning brought grey overcast skies and a miserable drizzle; the temperature had fallen to a more seasonal six degrees late-September norm. The eight mile ride from New Cross to the City was wet and cold and we both realised this wasn't going to be such an easy job after all; wouldn't cocktail bar waiting or revising history have been a better idea? The first fall of many was on Tuesday morning. Pedestrians were to be the biggest danger. Riding around the most populated streets in the country where people rely on only one of their senses at any time or some innate belief in their own inner radar, is very dangerous.

It is well known in the City that catching up with the FT whilst walking makes the reader immune to the usual courtesies that pedestrians give to one other; but what people won't realise is that the same Inner City slicker with his pink paper under his nose is so skilled that he or she (they were nearly all 'he's' then) is even able to negotiate a busy road using just their hearing; an incredible talent. Yes, we'd seen it so many times; can't hear a bus or a cab so must be safe enough to cross whilst simultaneously ingesting breakfast and Lex.

Now, this is all fine when a silently approaching cyclist has learned to read the minds and bodies of merger-mad bankers immersed in FT talk. But if they haven't, then the result is going to be painful for both. Before anything could be done to avert the collision, my left brake lever hit the pinstriped trader on his hip. This forced the brake to engage and instantly shred the tubular tyre from its rim. My rider went over the front and managed to embrace the startled stock-picker as they went to the ground together. I bounced my way painfully down the road. There was a moments silence as the street stood still; a silence very quickly filled with a tirade of expletives from my rider as he pulled himself embarrassedly away from the fallen pedestrian with the ripped suit and bloodied lacerations - the asphalt is much harder than it looks when you're knocked down by a speeding bicycle. Picking me up, my rider examined the bent front wheel and turned back to the city man.

"You're going to pay for this - where's your wallet?"

"But what about my suit?" The voice was weak with a pronounced whine, and the request sounded like he didn't expect to receive a positive answer.

"Where's your wallet? Get it out now!" The requisite banknotes were handed over and the two separated. We walked to the nearest bike shop for a new tubular tyre and the humbled young slicker retired to the safety of his office with bloody knees and even bloodier indignation. My surprisingly aggressive rider had been unhurt by the incident, but the forcefulness of his anger and his intimidating manner surprised everyone that witnessed it; there must be something about riding a bike fast and then falling off which causes the fight or flight response to favour the former; the banker was twice his size. Even I was surprised, as I'd never seen him be like that before; and it turned out not to be the last time. In his words they 'were all out to kill him'.

Despite what is said about the dangers of cycling in London, we did find it to be an efficient way to earn a few bob. Once we were up and running and got to know how to get the deliveries done quickly with as little hanging around as was necessary, we were doing nigh-on 100 miles a day. Punctures were rare and really close shaves occurred only once or twice a day; they were actually pretty exciting and usually involved a calculated risk that paid off. Buses and lorries are slow moving beasts which largely do what you expect of them; the unpredictability of a Black cab u-turn makes it, conversely, a highly predictable event - if you see a fare get in from the pavement, then within ten seconds the cab will move away and either go straight on or do a u-turn; it's what they do; people shouldn't be surprised.

But pedestrians are another case. Pedestrians have plenty of opportunities to cross roads safely using Zebra or Pelican crossings but, no, they insist on taking their chances where and whenever it pleases them. Paid heaps to beat the market means that City workers had lost all sense of personal responsibility and deemed that everyone had to stop for them because they were 'entitled' to cross the road; they took risks with millions of pounds every day; crossing roads was nothing. We genuinely hated pedestrians; we didn't ride on their pavements so they shouldn't walk on our roads!

The BT pager came to dominate our lives. It was the only source of work and therefore, money; every little beep meant more money. He recorded all the jobs on a special sheet provided by the fat controller, but once it was handed in he had no record of what he had done. The company decided how much he was paid and there was no breakdown; he just accepted what they said - he studied history; he always got more than he expected so he believed whatever he was told.

It is important to remember that this all happened in 1984 when there were no big brother CCTV cameras to watch our every move and a time when the British public had largely fallen out of love with the Victorian bicycle; drivers hadn't yet learned to hate the lycra clad, middle aged proles on their carbon machines who dogged the cities in the early part of the following century. It was the year when the Austin Maestro was Britain's second best-selling car and the tatty old pound note was withdrawn after 150 years in circulation - well they weren't actually that old, but they were tatty. Despite all this the 1980's was a great time to be a bicycle because you were largely ignored and frequently alone on the road; other road users just thought you were slightly nuts; and no one ever tried to steal a fixed wheel bike. Also, nobody jumped the lights and there were no cycle lanes or big boxes at the lights to give you a head start and annoy the drivers; we were the curious sideshows that hovercrafts and C5's would eventually be. How were we to know that we were both behind and ahead of the times? But the thing that made cycling so much safer then was the lack of mobile phones; drivers only had the radio or a C90 compilation to distract them.

The pedestrian crashes kept coming and we escaped injury and serious damage every time through pure luck. There was the Greek man near Trafalgar Square who was angrily hauled in front of a policeman outside St Martin's when his offer of a handful of Drachmas (there was no such thing as Euros) was refused as compensation; the sage old bobby suggested that sterling might appease the crazy cyclist, and Stelios took the hint and emptied another pocket; another new wheel.

The young woman in Oxford Street got no less sympathy than the rest of them. She even looked before stepping off the kerb in front of us; we hit her very hard. I think from her screams that she probably broke her wrist when she went down, but we were late for a pickup and were able to keep upright, so didn't stop. She was quickly forgotten. It didn't pay to dwell.

As the weeks went by, and our traffic skills improved, so the more chances we took; rapidly closing gaps in the traffic were a speciality and many a motorcycle dispatcher was dropped through the middle of traffic moving in both directions. Dirt-stained shoulders from running along the sides of grimy London buses were common in the cold dark winter streets. Christmas was approaching and the money was good. He didn't want to stop; the stone broke student was going to buy the best Christmas ever.

He started to push for the jobs. The fitter he got, the faster we went, the more money we earned. The moves that were once risky were now safe, a sure bet even. The traffic seemed to slow down in our presence and we simply flowed through in our endless mission to deliver. Every day got easier as we battled through the cold, the rain and the slippery roads. He was even learning to shout warnings to pedestrians. We were on fire; even the fat controller began to appreciate our incredible work rate.

We probably would have made it to Christmas it if we hadn't tried that manoeuvre on Victoria Street. Yes, we were in a hurry. We had the right of way to overtake the bus at the bus stop, but if he had just thought about the passengers exiting from the rear of bus in front and how they might just walk straight across the road through the stationary traffic? We hit four of them in one go. A record, yes, but an expensive and painful one. Concussion, a broken right wrist and collar bone, dirty lacerations to the left side of his face, and another bent wheel. He looked a mess and, like the pedestrians we hit, he was going to be sore for Christmas. Band Aid was going to be of no help to any of them. I was fine, bar a couple more scratches and my front wheel. Everyone got home eventually, and no one made a claim - no one did in those days. But Christmas and the remainder of the winter were quiet for me. A bit of a relief really; it could have been far worse.

Ride to Haiku

Ride the urban maze?

Commute angry city roads?

Cyclists, don't dare doze!

Cars can't hurt cyclist

Don't crash on their own, but

Drivers still get pissed.

Leave the towns to ride

Cross the counties far and wide

See it! - here's a guide

Surrey's golden falls

Guttered leaves rustle 'neath

Sunday cycling tours

Hampshire's hedged lanes hide

Secret by-ways, rambling hills

All terrains to ride.

Shropshire's tarmac hosts

Whole day time trials; steely men

Vie to mile the most

Lancs men of the mills

Racing to top o' th' fields

First up wins the spills

Check out Cromer's pier

Meet wind and waves; turn home

Coast long roads, big gear.

Kent's green garden cloaks

Bluebell woods long back-road routes

Fresh air, wind in spokes

Wales' highest spike

Pen-y-Pass tests man and bike

Best to ride not hike

Night ride cross Dartmoor

Glimpse the deer, see the light at

Sun rise, Staple Tor

Oxford's roads crumbling

Bike lanes patchy, breached and holed

Steer clear a tumbling!

Blue Boris cycle

Slowly gaining affection

Ride's quite delightful

Lincolns pancake flat

Ride all day, ne'er change gear, but

Watch for imps 'n' that

Yorks is hard, no doubt

Big tough 'ills that stop at nowt,

Needs legs strong and stout

Jurassic coast trip

Big fossil cliffs, blue sea view

Dorset's tourist strip

Avebury stands alone

Wiltshire's wheel-like rings atone

Ride me to the stones?

Silver stones on road

In Northants, famous for speed,

Legend Sheene n'er slowed

Cavendish so fast

Wins stages off the front, but

Manxman oft downcast

Brad's the peoples man

Britain's modist tour de force

Gold Olympian!

Site of GB Golds

London's Velopark lavished

Battling cyclists goals

Builders want to buy

Herne Hills outdoor cycling track

Legends won't come back...

Cambridge bikes are slow

Book-laden beasts of burden

Blues blades win rows, though

Take the Highlands roads

See trees, Lochs Fyne and Ness

Landscapes that impress

Ride round your Britain

Remember what you see, cos

Times are a changin'

Hot Ride

I never quite knew whether I was better off being owned or stolen, but having been in both camps I'm entitled to a view. Being originally bought and owned by James had its positives; complete adoration from a weak-kneed banker, dry rides, plenty of time indoors hung on the wall as a work of art for dinner party debate, and even the occasional overseas trip. But the downsides probably outweighed them; heavily overweight rider, inappropriate set-up (well, certainly for a bike of my class), inattentive home servicing which amounted to no more than regular Muc-Off Bike Cleaner rub downs….didn't he know about air pressures, brake adjustment and chain replacement? I'm the cycling equivalent of a formula-one car you know? I need top levels of care and attention, and I do not need 28mm section tyres!

The day I was stolen was quite amusing. James had taken me on his usual Saturday morning sixty minute ride to the café in Windsor where he met up with his group of cycling friends and had cake and coffee - for at least two hours - before riding me home. I'd been left leaning against a low wall in all my technological glory and in full view of the sun for an hour or so - my tyres had been a bit low when we'd started out but, due to the intense heat from the direct sunlight, they were now fit to burst. James and the others were, as usual, sitting about ten feet away on the other side of the café railings and chatting about banking and wives and children. I noticed the young man with pale skin walking towards me; he was looking at me with an intensity I'd not seen before. At first, I thought he must be looking at my wireless SRAM shifters and my pro-level hydraulic disc brakes, and, probably, my monocoque carbon frame swathed with Pinarello decals; but principally I think his shrewd little eyes realised that I wasn't locked up. I was free to be taken by whoever wanted me. Ninety-three kilos of fat banker in Speedplay cleat-shod cycling shoes would take an age to even get to his feet, let alone chase anyone making off with me.

In the event, James didn't even notice that I had gone until I was a hundred metres up the road; I thought he'd been looking after me better than that. Terry my abductor, simply walked me away. It was better than funny.

So what was it like being stolen? Well, initially it was a bit dull; I was taken to a garage and left for a couple of weeks somewhere in Windsor. Terry, had finally ridden me away from the cafe after James decided he would put in a spirited chase on foot - now that was genuinely hilarious! James really wasn't a runner - just seeing him try was frame shakingly funny - but the sublime moment was when one of his cleats slid on a dog turd and his huge lycra-sheathed backside ended up on top of it. I laughed so much my chainring teeth rattled. It turned out my time with Terry, wasn't exactly a step up from James; he didn't clean me or service me either - nor did he put air in my tyres.

So I guess I might have been looking a little bit sorry for myself when a couple of people were brought in to look at me.

"I just bought 'er on the ride to work scheme and, well, I never used 'er much so I'm selling 'er." This was Terry's line to what turned out to be prospective buyers from somewhere called Gumtree.

"I'll give you £250 tops mate."

"Nah - these things is worth a mint - it cost me five and half grand, you know."

"£500 - no more."

"£600 and you got a deal." I couldn't believe it. I was only a year old and I had all the leading edge technology available for a bicycle - and I was being sold for just ten per cent of my original cost! Madness.

Well, they obviously decided to do a 'deal' and I was then taken away to a better garage in Reading where I was left for another couple of weeks and where, at least, they put some air in my Conti's. Soon there were more people, and more haggling - this time they were from another place I didn't know either - Ebay?

"I've had 'er bike a couple of years - I did the Etape - you know, in France? - then me knee went so I'm just not able to go out any more. I'll take £2,000 - I think she is worth every penny - and that's a lot less than I paid for her I can tell you." It seemed a strange thing to say because my new owner who was a lot smaller than James hadn't so much as even sat on me; his feet wouldn't have reached the pedals.

Well, I am still stolen, of course, but now, at least, I have an owner that actually wants to ride me properly and who probably doesn't know I was stolen. I was bought by Charlie's Dad who couldn't afford to buy a new bike as good as me but knew that his son was a 'prospect' so he needed to get the best he could for him.

This season we've been competing in races at the Hillingdon circuit in West London and Charlie is starting to win; he's even got a coach. So he's good, and even their mechanic looks after me properly. I think me and Charlie could go places. Sadly, the other bikes won't talk to me because they know I'm stolen. So it's not all good.

24 Hours

In the darkness he can just make out his forearms; flat and bare on the bars, glistening with baubles of sweat; a powerful white light spears through the cables under his hands spreading its lumens across the smooth Shropshire tarmac; 14 hours in and 10 more to go. Fear? No, not for the dark; fear is reserved for the midnight puncture puck or the onset of premature exhaustion brought about by failing to fuel – easily done in the first frantic hours of the previous day. The tunnel-like world of the night exists for six hours but it is the time when 24 hour time trials are won and, more frequently, lost. There are always quicker riders, but if they can't fight through the night then they lose.

It's at this time that many riders feel their body start to stiffen and their will weaken; sleep besieges their thoughts with tender memories of rest and warmth; end it all now; take to your bed; stop the pain. But this is my rider's time - this is when he gets stronger. The roads are empty and lonely bar the occasional unidentifiable light beam on the opposite carriageway, and yet he feels more lucid and on track than at any time in the race; now is the time for us to push; I'm smiling in the dark at the sheer thrill of staying out on the road when everyone else has gone to their beds. The excitement of the first few hours when the supporters still cheered has long gone, and the pace has settled; but we're still racing, we're still time trialling; his body is still stretched across me as it would be for a 10 or a 25 miler. He's not one of the speed merchants who blitz the Sunday mornings before breakfast, he's one of the endurance men and women who ride through the day, and then the night, and then the day again.

So how does the long distance triallist cope with hours and hours in the saddle? How does he distance his head from his unseen opponents? Support crews gossiping in the night with tales of abandons and bonking competitors try to help; but their words hardly register in the befuddled minds of athletes stopping only briefly to refuel. He can only think of himself and his need to keep on moving, keep up the speed, keep on the road. In truth, he'd rather not stop, but he needs to know he's not the only man left in that dark, unforgiving place; he needs to look into sympathetic eyes.

Bikes like me are loved and despised equally. No bikes are more fettled, more measured, more adjusted or tuned; optimised for the opposing demands of aero efficiency and long distance comfort, we're the ultimate cycling compromise. Too aero and we'll break the rider's body within four hours; to comfortable and he'll be slow. After the race he'll hate me; the pain of this day takes a long time to heal.

During the summer nights the temperature can be surprisingly low, but my rider is still working hard and consuming enough fuel to generate his own heat; in the crisp dark air his sweat drips onto my bars and into the food tray; carb-laden cubes of bread pudding and banana bread regularly and reluctantly stuffed in and swallowed whole; this engine needs its fuel like a steam train needs its coal. The monotony of breathing timed subconsciously with his cadence, bores me for hours.

Periodically I find myself smiling like a madman because I know what's coming; the large Quina Brook roundabout where a few hardy supporters sit around for the night under the streetlights and gently clap as the competitors, still down on the bars, spear out of the darkness on one of the few downhill slopes to execute the irregular 360 turn - the speeds are high and the thrill intense - before disappearing again onto the 40 mile circuit. After all this time I know the road, the bumps, the building excitement for the sunrise - although I know he'll get low in those late night hours when the sun refuses to rise above the horizon; it seems to be deliberate. But now is the night and the night is our time.

24 hour time trials are an allegory for a man's life on earth; in the first six hours he bursts from the start with speed, verve and a hope that represents the promise of a young child growing into an adult; an entrance then tempered during the second six hours when the reality and potential futility of his mission become clear – so much work still has to be done; such a long way to go; the body's beginning to hurt. But success or failure is determined in the night; similarly, middle age determines what a man will really achieve when the going gets tough – the big distance men and women don't sleep and rarely stop for supplies in the night; the big milers, the real contenders, are rarely young and predominantly inward people. And then, as the last six hours unfold, only those who've ridden the night with the willpower and determination to keep up the pace and the pain, make the grade. Every one of them collapses on the stroke of 24 - a private, painful passing by the side of the road - they beg forgiveness for their folly and their joy at finishing; the tears of exhaustion are short-lived but real. The 24 hour time triallers give their soul to their bike and take only a mileage as reward. They are the cyclists that truly know how to suffer.

The Chain Gang

Dear Cyclist

We are the Chain Gang. We might not be an officially recognised organisation or even a nefarious underground bunch of miscreants doing bad deeds, but we do represent a very powerful and progressive movement with a very important message for everyone that rides a bike. In fact, this missive is so important that if you're a regular cyclist and you don't read it and then pass it on to at least five other cyclists, then you will be forever pushing your pedals uphill; you will be forever slow, and forever late. You have been warned!

Our message is simple. Your bicycle chain is the most important mechanical part of your bike and one which requires constant attention and care; as Karl Marx nearly said, 'cyclists of the world unite; you have nothing to lose but your chains.'

When we started this letter, we didn't think we needed to explain exactly what your chain does, but it appears that there are more of you than we thought that have somehow failed to notice the relevance of the thin little black wobbly thing connecting your pedals to your back wheel. So here is a short summary of what it is and what it does:

Your bicycle chain is a mechanical device known as a roller chain, and it transfers the power from your pedals to the rear wheel of your bicycle in the most mechanically efficient way; forget drive shafts and gear wheels; forget toothed belts (they have their advantages, but efficiency isn't one of them); forget levers and cams. Chains are by far and away the best solution! It is for good reason that the fastest motorbikes still have chains, and why cars waste so much of their power - OK, so this missive is about the transmission rather than the power unit, so let's stick to the message! Just believe us on this one.

Now, before you think that we're going to rail on at you about oiling your chain, then don't fret, because we're not. There has been too much written and proscribed and preached about the 'best' way to lubricate your chain and they are probably all correct. But it is worth knowing that a new chain is efficient whether it is lubricated or not because its mechanical efficiency is all that counts - laboratory tests have shown that lubrication makes absolutely no difference at all to a new chain. The difference that a lack of lubrication will make, however, is simply the amount of time that an un-oiled chain will remain efficient; it will wear out very quickly.

And here is the crux! Most people ride around on bicycle chains that are worn and so are therefore inefficient - a lot of them even have oil on them! Inefficient chains mean you go slower, and mean your bike goes slower and means you will always be late; be it to work or to the end of your race (you will more likely lose!).

So we in the Gang maintain that the 457 separate parts - yes, the 114 outer plates, 114 inner plates, 114 rollers and 114 link pins in the average multi-geared bike chain (if your chain is old then they have 114 bushes as well) - that make up your chain, and, coincidentally, represent more than half of all the parts in your whole bicycle, are worth looking after properly. And don't just think this means that you have to oil the darned thing every time you go out, because that can be even worse than doing nothing. Oiling a dirty chain - and, by the way, they are hung in a place behind the front wheel where they pick up every droplet of water and speck of dust and grime from the road - is probably as bad an idea as doing nothing at all. Grit is the killer of chains. Grit will get inside the rollers and between the plates, and, with every turn of the pedal, a tiny bit more of these parts will be ground away. Grit wears down the teeth on your sprockets, the teeth on your chain wheel, your plates and your rollers, your pins and your jockeys. It will reduce the efficiency to that of a piece of string; and then it will break - proving that the weakest link is in fact the strongest because just one little link has power enough to make you walk home in the rain.

Let's take a break from this tirade for a moment. Let us take you back to the summer of 2012 when the Olympic movement came to London and the British cyclists claimed a chestful of medals on the road and the track. One thing is absolutely certain. King Bradley's chain was clean. It was so clean that you could have sat it on your settee - unlike your dog; it was so clean you could have introduced it to your grandmother - also unlike your dog. Keeping things clean was clearly going to be part of the mantra of Mr Brailsford's marginal gains philosophy, but it wasn't just to make things looks good and shiny for the TV cameras; keeping it clean meant that the mechanical bits were able to do what they were designed to do. Now, Dave probably didn't actually tell all the mechanics to make sure that Bradley's chain was cleaned just before they set him off for the time trial from the grounds of Hampton Court Palace, because the philosophy was embedded in everything they did, but you get the idea. We maintain that if having a clean chain made all the difference to the Gold medal time for Bradley, then surely it will get us to work just that little bit more quickly?

Once upon a time a lady called Rosa Luxemburg, who lived at a time when bicycles with chains were in their infancy, and who also happened to be a disciple of Mr Marx, took his train of thought a step further when she said, 'Those who do not move, do not notice their chains.' I think that says it all? Now pass this on and go and buy a new chain!

The War to End All Rides

We have been waiting for Charles to come home. Four years I've stood against these stairs; the occasional waft of Ariel's duster my only physical contact with anyone. Charles, respectful of every bicycle he met, would never have left me, especially me, outdoors. I live in the hallway. But when he went away everything changed. The staff have either been let go or they died in France. The War changed everything; Mrs Stone spends most days sat listless in the bay window looking across the sea from our house high above the Channel.

As a VÉLO FRANÇAIS, I consider myself a beautiful French creation - which is a little ironic since the company that manufactured me was founded in Germany. But at least I was made by a Frenchman, in France, in the COTE D'OR; the place where VIN EXTRAORDINAIRE is produced. Well, that is what my Charles always told everyone. As well as being a wine connoisseur and an appreciator of things most beautiful, Charles is also the 'Terrotiste' of Kent - you see, I'm a Terrot Racing bicycle and the PEDALEURS of our marque were given their own special name; we are best known for our beautiful lines and our extraordinary speed. As for Charles Douglas Stone, well, he wasn't quite so famous, but he was a CYCLISTE EXTRAORDINAIRE and was distantly related to the 2nd Baron of Cobham (of Kent, that is). More importantly, though, the H Company PELOTON of the territorial Kent Cyclist Battalion wouldn't have been the same without his imperious leadership.

Charles had always ridden bicycles and I was his favourite. *Charles m'a aimé.*

Things could have been so very different had he gone to India with the rest of the Kent Cyclist Battalion in 1916. Typical Charles. He didn't want to just protect the Kent coastal defences with the rest of his riding chums before they got their India call up. No, Captain Charles Stone volunteered for Imperial Service instead and so went to the Front in northern France. I knew why he felt he had to go, but I didn't agree with him; officers didn't ride bicycles at the Front.

I have been very patient, standing here, against the stairs in our Folkestone house. I always knew that he had gone away to do something important for his country; he said England expected it. But I never thought that it would take this long. The muffled quiet of the house has been interrupted only by the distant sound of the 'guns'; I don't know whose guns they were, I just knew that people were being hurt by them. The noise of guns came from across the Channel, but even here, next to the stairs, they sounded like they were just down the road in Sandgate or Hythe. Mrs Stone closed her eyes and winced when they were really bad. The relentless barrage of noise and the flashes in the distant night sky to the south fill the air with prophetic fear for hours and light up the hallway like an electrical storm; before falling silent, muzzled, again. House told me that she hated the quiet as much as the noise, because neither ever meant good news; we'll never forget the noiseless day we learned that Claude, the butler, had perished at Verdun; blown to smithereens by the Hun; his demise widowed his wife and permanently damaged his daughter.

We began to hear stories that Charles was back in England and that he was staying firstly in a place near London called Roehampton, and then, closer to us, at the Royal Pavilion in Brighton; I knew Charles would like the Royal connection, but I still didn't understand why he couldn't come home.

The other day, after reading a long letter in the hallway, Mrs Stone stood and looked at me; she usually just walked past slightly disdainfully; I'm not sure that she approved of the amount of time Charles and I had spent together away from the house before the war. Our jaunts, as he called them, had taken us all over Kent and we'd spent many a night at small Inns in the pretty fielded villages of the High Weald; the Vineyard in Lamberhurst and the Star and Eagle in Goudhurst were regular memorable stops for his weary legs. The ever-bombastic Charles had no problem meeting new people, and many a night was spent drinking hoppy beer with local pickers into the small hours, before climbing up winding wooden stairs to a meagre room over the bar. But the other day Mrs Stone didn't just look at me - she put her hand on my saddle and sighed. She seemed so sad about something.

It was clear that the War to end all wars had ended, but Charles still didn't come home. His family came and spoke with Mrs Stone in the drawing room in hushed whispers - as if not wanting me to hear what was being said. House told me that they just talked about how things would change when Charles eventually came home. They all seemed so sad and brought long-stemmed flowers for Mrs Stone. They were acting like Charles had died, although I knew he hadn't. I just wanted to be taken for a ride in the fresh Kentish air; I wanted to be out of the hall.

It was a Tuesday morning and I could see there was someone outside. The front door's frosted glass panels obscured most things, but not on a sunny day when people were stood, framed, by the path outside. Mrs Stone came quickly after the bell appealed for the door to be opened. She'd been getting ready all morning. I'd known that there was an excitement brewing for something, but I also knew that Mrs Stone had been crying a lot. She hadn't sat and looked out at the Channel for a while.

The door opened and there he was. It was my beautiful Charles. Sat, in a funny-looking chair with wheels, and a blanket over his lap he smiled thinly, wanly, as a tall man pushed him into the hall. Mrs Stone burst into loud tears and hugged him hard. I didn't know where to look. Thankfully, the tall man took him into the lounge with Mrs Stone before leaving them there together and quietly discharging himself; carefully recoiling the latch bolt in the door so as to shut it silently behind him. I could hear Charles comforting Mrs Stone. He didn't sound the same as before he left; he spoke slowly and deliberately; I detected a tremor. Charles had always been so ebullient and positive.

"It's alright Vera, dearest - I'm home now. It's such a relief to be here - there were times when I thought I would never see you again. I promise, now, that it's all going to be fine." His assurances didn't seem to stop Mrs Stone crying and I'm sure I heard a slight gasp of either pain or resignation from Charles.

Shortly afterwards Mrs Stone made them a pot of Earl Grey tea and she seemed to brighten up a bit.

As the sun reached its highest point of the day and the hallway floor glared white with the light, I heard his solid rubber wheels moving across the boards to the doorway of the lounge. Charles, looking as gaunt as Lincoln's memorial, came out, silhouetted against the sunlight; the wheels of his chair turning gently in his hands. He stopped close to me.

"I'm going to miss you," he murmured. He put his hand on my front wheel and lowered his head. Tears dropped quietly onto the blanket and melted into the wool. "Oh God, why did this have to happen to us."

The blanket, its corner caught slightly under the single front wheel of his chair, slipped down to the floor. Charles had no legs.

Ball of Fire

Every weekday morning at around seven thirty, me and 'Angry Ash' (as I called him) embarked on a very special race. One in which we were the only competitor. We raced nothing more than the time and the little numbers on the computer - they were the sole arbiter of success or failure. For three years, the daily race to and from the office consumed Ash.

But I think he misunderstood. I think he thought that commute meant he could change a bicycle ride to work into a daily time trial; the outcome being that thirty-six year old Ash treated everyone else on the road with complete and utter contempt - because they were either not in his race or they were getting in the way of his hot ride.

"Hey buddy - what's with your rider?" It was another carbon road bike, a Cannondale, whose owners are invariably easy going. The particular rider in question had just sheepishly shuffled his bike sideways after having been scolded by the ever-combustible Ash whilst we all waited at the red light. "He's very rude, you know."

"Yes, who does he think he is?" Squeaked the pink Pendleton ladies bike with the wicker basket near the kerb; most other commuters treated her lady rider with the sort of respect that the art dealer from Mayfair was accustomed to; Ash, though, had bellowed at her rudely on several occasions previously.

"If I were you, I'd crash!" Now there was an amusing idea; Brompton's always have a sparky sense of humour - I guess they need to with such small wheels.

"Mate!" I knew, without even looking, that it was the steel fixie bike whose rider was often a target for Ash's scorching abuse when he pulled away too slowly from a set of lights, "mate, one day my rider is goin' do one to your guy - he takes the biscuit!" It sounded like a threat but I didn't know what he thought he could do. Ash and I were quick - not the quickest - but on a good day we'd toast anyone. Not many could keep up with us on the Embankment - and certainly not the fat-tyred fixie.

The comments that day from the other bikes weren't out of the ordinary; Ash had already issued commands to three mere 'commuters' who'd inadvertently strayed from their line at our first major set of lights; this was the set where the Garmin was given the 'Go'; where Ash felt he'd warmed up enough - warming up was what he did in the first mile of the ride from the Common.

"Come on guys, you know what he's like - it's just the way he is." I was fed up with making excuses for him but I actually enjoyed the attention. It wasn't me that was rude.

"That's not an excuse - you mean he is <u>always</u> like this?" Pendleton was as indignant as ever.

"Yes, he is." fixie wasn't letting up, "and one day someone's goin' to put him out!"

I had to be the most hated bike in South West London. And do you know what? Ash didn't even belong to a club or have any cycling friends. We never went for rides at the weekends or on the summer evenings like other bikes. As well as only ever riding alone, I think he lived alone; in fact, I think I was his only real friend. As you might imagine, Ash never told me why he seemed to be in such a hurry - a particularly perceptive hybrid once said that Ash was probably very lonely; I think it was wishful thinking from the ugly hybrid. But Ash's disdain for the other riders was palpable. I guess he talked with people when he was at work or at home in his flat - I was left in the underground parking - but when we were on the road, he never spoke to anyone.

I'm big for a bike - my frame is a 61 - and Ash is big too; not overly muscled, but long, lean and sinewy. The tall, pinched contours of his face, set hard from the constant effort of pushing his legs to the limit, was all that was seen by most other riders; a prominent adam's apple matched the bump on his nose.

The ride that day took its usual course. Deep breaths on the line before accelerating away from the lights; then timing our runs to get the maximum chance of making the green traffic lights - while still abusing everyone in our way. Pedestrian crossings meant nothing to Ash - people crossing them were there to be dodged; it seemed like he thought they were doing it on purpose to slow us down. A week or so back, there were two bikes waiting next to a van as an elderly man with a dog crossed Chelsea's Kings Road. Ash wasn't going to stop and barged his way through the two bikes and in front of the man; who then proceeded, walking-stick aloft, to berate the other two cyclists.

"You're all the same you lot - no respect!" Once he'd got to the pavement, one of the riders decided to have it out with Ash and manfully gave chase and caught us at a later set of lights before the right turn on to the Embankment.

"Hey you - who do you think you are?" Ash didn't bother to look - he never said anything when someone spoke to him. "Hey! What's your problem - you can't treat people like that?" Ash was watching the traffic light sequence with his usual intensity and simply rode away on the stroke of the amber with the other rider left standing dumbfounded in the middle of the road. I gave a nonchalant look back at his pretty little Colnago. We were off again and picked up the regular south westerly tail as we joined the road along the Thames Embankment. The speed went up. Deftly moving into the stream of cars, we drafted up to 30 miles an hour before switching to the centre of the road as the traffic slowed for the next set of red lights. Perfect timing; we blazed through the standing hoardes of cyclists as the lights went amber. Ash was on fire; we knew how to nail this stretch.

I was brought up in a factory where everyone started out largely the same. The bikes were given different levels of trim - some had carbon this and carbon that, and others were made for a 'lower price point'. But underneath, we were all from the same factory and all of us were made by the same group of people. Everyone got on and no one really cared about how different we looked on the outside. Being sold to a person was deemed to be the highlight of our lives - just to be wanted and loved by a cyclist was all we craved. Once I was bought and taken out of the shop and away from the other unsold bikes I became conscious how different other bikes looked to me and how being owned by a person changed us all. Most bikes lost the personalities they'd had in the factory where we all treated each other in a friendly way. They had been subsumed into the men and women who sat on their saddles. I'm pretty sure that Pendleton didn't talk with that accent in the factory in Taiwan - and fixie sounded as if he'd been playing street polo for years, when I knew for a fact that he been bought from Evans Cycles only six months previously. But, strangely, they didn't seem to have a choice - their owners controlled them; they caressed them; they abused them; they won or lost races with them; bikes became just like their owners. It wasn't the same with me though; I was the same bike I'd always been. I might have enjoyed being ridden by him, but I thought Ash was a cretin like everyone else.

When something quite unbelievable happened that day I realised it was because, from the outset, I had been made slightly differently. It was because of me that the events of that sunny morning on the Embankment resulted in Ash becoming, well, more like everyone else. I still don't know if it was just how I felt about him at the time, or if it was just me wanting to be liked by all the other bikes; but I know the outcome changed everything.

We were sat at the lights on the entrance to Parliament Square - our time was good that day - Ash, hot, alert and counting the seconds to the next change, was blowing hard. I was looking ahead; away from the other bikes as they drew alongside; some of them had been shouted at by him only minutes previously as we sped past them.

"Keep left!", "Coming through!", Idiot!" It was all perfectly normal for our ride to work.

Still looking ahead so as not to catch the eye of any of the other bikes, I saw an old woman on the other side of the square; I noticed her faltering walk - no one walking around Parliament Square at 7.45am ever faltered; this was the place for leaders and flunkies. Everyone is important when they walk around Parliament Square before nine - something was wrong. As the lights changed and we moved forwards, I did something that I never done before - I momentarily squeezed my head bearings tight. I still don't know why I did it but Ash's balance was slightly thrown as the steering refused to turn and his foot missed its connection with the pedal; I felt myself giggle. He cursed out loud and pushed away again. This time I relaxed the gear cable enough to let the gear slip down a cog or two. Now we were being overtaken by all the other commuters. Ash smarted and piled huge pressure onto the pedals and, within seconds, we were ahead of them. As we rounded the first bend of the square the old woman came into view once again. Then, with all the effort I could produce, I squeezed my brake blocks onto the rims - which is really hard to do! Now I was laughing inside.

Suddenly, I was aware that Ash, though manfully trying to oppose my unexpected braking, had seen her too. I knew it because I felt the pressure ease through the pedals and his hands lighten on the bars. Did seeing her bring back a recollection of something? Ash stared unblinkingly across the square. We slowed. Surely, my little games didn't mean that he was actually going to stop - Ash never stopped. The bent-over figure stopped too, and an ashen face looked up with pearly eyes. At that moment, her foot faltered at the edge of a paving stone and she collapsed forwards onto the pavement. None of the other pedestrians seemed to notice her; one even stepped over her feet as he continued on his executive journey.

We stopped next to the kerb and Ash dismounted.

"What's up - got a flat? Ha ha - couldn't happen to a bigger loser!" Fixie passed by with a steely grin and a swaggering cadence. There wasn't time to reply.

Ash, clearly oblivious, was towering over her. Surprisingly tenderly, he lifted her grey hand and spoke to her.

"Are you OK love? - do you hurt?" His voice was softer than I had ever heard it. I could see her smile a little and shake her head from side to side.

"If I could just sit down for a moment?" Ash looked around. As he did so, he realised that a small posse of people had suddenly surrounded them. Someone pushed through importantly.

"Excuse me - I'm a nurse?" Before Ash could say anything, the bystanders became helpers and he was slowly removed away from her as if a man wearing lycra shouldn't be so close. He stood watching helplessly as they took over.

"Will she be OK?" Please?"

"Yes, there's nothing to see now - she'll be fine - no need to stare." After a minute he seemed to realise that there was nothing more he would be allowed to do, so he walked back to me.

The rest of the ride into work was slow. The Garmin was switched to 'Off' and I felt a genuine chilling in Ash. This wasn't him. That evening ride home was similarly slow and he spoke to no one. None of the other bikes spoke to me either - even those that knew me. It was as if they knew something had happened - well, either that or they just didn't notice us when we were riding slowly like the rest of them.

I never found out why the fire went out in Ash. Yes, I had tried to sabotage his ride just after I saw the old lady, but I didn't 'make' him stop. But we never raced into work again.

I miss the daily race. No one ever talks to me anymore. We're just commuters, like all the others, going through the daily drudgery of riding to work. Sometimes, on the way home, we stop at a small block of flats opposite Battersea Power Station and Ash knocks on a door. The little old lady from Parliament Square always opens the door with the same question.

"Hello my love - fancy a cup of tea?"

Village Bike

Wow, he was a bit of a rough one! It's a good job they're not all like that or I wouldn't have lasted a week. The 'he' in question picked me up outside the station at around three this afternoon and without so much as a single word, checked me out for size, gave my saddle a squeeze and took me to a house up Duke Street; the one where the lovely pregnant lady lives; I say lovely, because she always rides me so nicely and talks to me all the time. I think the man was in a hurry because he didn't even tuck his trousers in his socks and the flared bits kept getting caught in the chain; pity there wasn't any oil left on it to dirty them. Once we got to the house, he leant me against the garden hedge, before marching up to and hammering on the front door with his fist. I should have known something was awry as it was such a strange time to get picked up; I usually get the weekday afternoons to myself.

During that first ride he was really beastly to me, you know. At one point, when we were stopped at the lights in the High Street on the way to Duke Street, he started thumping his hand on the handlebars. It wasn't as if something was loose or he was trying to adjust anything; he just thumped my bars and muttered to himself. Then, when my rear mudguard stay started rattling against the wheel - it had been loose for a while since the three-eighths bolt rattled itself free when Mrs Maybrick from Florence Cottage was taking me to the chemist - he leapt off and started kicking at my rear wheel and saying horrible things. It didn't stop the rattling which started up instantly again as soon as we moved off.

The nice old man from the church, the Reverend Stainer, did try to fix the missing bolt with some green garden wire a while back, but that soon wore through and dropped off; I was actually quite pleased at the time, because the green didn't go so well with my colour; us Raleigh Wayfarers were painted navy blue. The Reverend is someone else that is always nice to me and sometimes takes me with him up the steep hill to see his brother on a Thursday afternoon, where afterwards they take tea in the garden. Usually, my afternoons are quiet through the week. The hills, by the way, are fine for me, as my Sturmey Archer AW 3-speed hub still works as well as it did when we left the Triumph Road factory in Nottingham in 1987.

A long time ago I used to belong Mr Roper at number 67 Rook Lane and he looked after me really well; I got a yearly service at Mr Evan's bicycle shop in the High Street where all my bearings were checked, my spokes were felt (the loose ones were tightened, which was always nice) and my brakes adjusted. Over the ten years we were together, he replaced my saddle once, and my brake and gear cables three times. My tyres were changed every year because Mr Brown rode me six miles out and back every day to the neighbouring town of Kings Worthy where he worked as a solicitor; they were always the same tyres; Michelin World Tour tyres with the amber walls. Size; 26 x 1 3/8 inches.

Then, one day, we had the accident. A red car pulled straight out of Lovedon Lane and hit Mr Roper and me. His leg took most of the impact from the car and we were thrown across the road where he landed on his head. He died and I never saw him again; so much for wearing his silly yellow helmet. After the accident I was taken to the police station in Winchester with a few dents and scratches, and hey left me there in the yard for over a year. I was billeted with some other bicycles, police bicycles, I think - all black and upright with rod brakes and black leather saddlebags. None of them spoke to me, which was a bit mean - it wasn't my fault that Mr Roper died. At least I was under cover at the station although some of the chrome on my handlebars went a little yellow.

When I was finally 'released', I ended up being ridden by nearly everyone in the village at one time or another. I don't know quite how I got back here, but I think one of the policemen rode me back after a 'late one' and just left me in the High Street. Thankfully my trusty dynamo lights still work so regular late night rides with the local boys aren't as dangerous as they could be - I do so enjoy the country lanes around the village in the dark. Recently, one of them from Larkwhistle Farm has got to taking me into Winchester at the weekends so that he can get back late without a using a taxi - they cost so much, you know. He is usually a bit drunk on the way home and we have to veer all over the road which is actually quite funny really - and even more so when he's got some juicy plum of a girl perched on my crossbar!

So, anyway, this 'man' who left me in the garden; the one who threw me in the hedge? He only left me there for a bit but when he came out he seemed to be in even more of a hurry than before - there had been lots of shouting from inside the house which ended when a woman screamed very loudly. Immediately after, he came out of the front door, picked me up and tried to ride me straight out of the drive. Now that was never going to work - Michelin World Tours weren't made for riding on gravel and we quickly fell down. Cursing loudly, he picked me up again and literally ran me to the road where he jumped on my saddle and hammered his feet on the pedals down the hill - I think he was taking me back the station. As our speed picked up he started to say really rude things about the pregnant lady - I tried not listen. But when he said something about the baby not being his 'so she deserved what she got' I became angry. I realised then that he was talking about that lovely lady with the yellow hair. What had he just done to her? She couldn't have 'deserved' anything.

We zoomed to the bottom of the hill in no time at all and, as we approached the T-junction with the man still cussing loudly, I decided that enough was enough; he needed to be taught a lesson. Wouldn't it be quite funny if the brakes didn't work and we were to career across the junction and into the bushes on the other side? That would teach him!

How was I to know that my favourite farm boy from Larkwhistle Farm was coming along the main road in the big red tractor with two comely girls in his cab? I think I might have taught my rider more than just a lesson; He died too.

Spin Cycle

Our days are long and the spin classes repetitive and boring. Apparently, I'm one of the 'lucky' ones because I'm sat in the front row which means that I get used in more sessions than the others. It actually means that I get the really keen customers - the ones who want to impress the trainer? The ones that try harder and sweat more? You know the type.

Of all the things that I'm unhappy about, customer sweat is the one thing I really hate. Glutinous, briny excretions from unmentionable pores that get liberally leaked over my frame, squeezed into my cushioned foam bars and slid over my silica infused saddle; noxious discharges from un-heavenly orifices. I hate the incessant drippings of that liquid exhaust from our spinners.

One of the guys from the back row told me recently that he is lucky if he gets ridden twice a day. Twice a day? I have someone sat whirling away on me for a minimum 12 of the 14 hours that Leeds' Total Spin Studio is open every day; every day, that is, of the seven days of the week that we have customers; and one week just rolls into the next; it never stops. OK, so we are regularly serviced and I've had my saddle and pedals upgraded a couple of times, but it still doesn't stop the relentless spinning spinning spinning and sweating sweating sweating. Even when they clean the floor after closing - and the floor really needs a clean after the Gatorade, the Powerade, the spittle and phlegm congeal to a pump-squeaking gum - even after the cleaning, I always end up back at the front!

You might think that Dave who runs the place would deem it a good idea to give us front-rowers a bit of a break occasionally and move things round a bit? No. Honestly, I don't think he thinks about anything much. You might also think that the cleaners would take offence at the salty crusts of desiccated sweat that form like cold fat in a pan along the bottom of my unseen underside. But no, they don't care either.

So are there any perks to being a spin bike? Well, there are a couple; they are usually in their mid twenties and wearing the thinnest lycra pants designed more for yoga rather than spinning. Oh yes, and the real bonus is that they tend not to sweat so much. The sweet-scented honey's always turn up for Lee's sessions; Lee has more muscles than the other trainers, and Lee gets the prettiest customers with the cutest bottoms filling his front row. They're content that their slender speeds and lacklustre endeavours will never bother the red zone, although Lee has been known to boost their little beating hearts with a simple pectoral flex. Front-rowers, like me, get pleasure from their gentle pelvic pulsing from above -the downside of this being that we don't get to watch them in their lycra pants; rows two and three seem get that view.

So who are the cursed customers that sweat? Who are the front-rowers that pound out their sessions in a frenzied fury with the least style or consideration for their fellow spinners? Some of them, to give them their due, are properly trained athletes that compete in triathlons and bike races and stuff - they're the ones that always have a better 'feel' with the pedals; they generate their power right round the pedal cycle rather than just at the front bit. Others, untrained, unpleasant and blissfully arrogant, are slightly strange people who just come to the studio to 'improve their fitness' and, seemingly, mark their progress by how much they can max their peak power output for five seconds or minimise their resting heart rate when they wake in the morning. Very odd people. These are the drippers. These are the spinners who never clean up after a session as if leaving half of their bodily fluids running down my flanks is a mark of their superior exertive prowess. It's not, and for what it's worth, it does nothing for my bearings when their sticky discharges seep deep into my inner private parts.

So how does Total Spin Studio rank among the other spin studios in the area? I obviously haven't been to any of the others, but I have heard what customers say whilst they're warming up. Apparently, the instructors here 'take you to another place' - well Lee clearly does. Here at Total Spin they are all 'Schwinn Certified', which, I think, means that they have passed a test so they know how to teach people to use us Schwinn spin bikes. They certainly shout a lot, so perhaps that is a big part of the certification process. There is also lots of 'crazy' music. Now, I understand from what people say, that all the spin studios have music, but apparently it is louder here and the beats are not just 'bigger' but are timed to go with the cadence of the pedals. Well, that's what they think, but, as far as I'm concerned, very few of the spinners are able to time their spinning with the music.

I heard the other day that the studio was in trouble. The story, from one of the guys on the back row who rarely has anyone sat on him, is that times are lean - not like the customers he gets in the back row then! But his story has started to be repeated by guys from the fifth row and even the fourth and third. It seems that Leeds is falling out of love with spinning; perhaps they all bought real bikes. Perhaps the roads up on the Moors are proving more of a draw than the sweat-filled fug of the Total Spin Studio. I blame the Grand Depart in 2014.

So what if the club closes down? Someone said they would sell us all off. What would that mean? What if one of the drippers bought me? I would have to lie about his cadence and mis-state his heart rate; I'd have to try to burn him out. But, and you never know, I could always get bought by one of Lee's lovely lasses. I'd be happy if one of them could take me home and sit and spin her little backside off on me for the rest of my life. Now that would be the way to go.

El Aurens

"Chaps, I have something tell you. If you could all gather round it would be lovely - no? OK, then I will just have to speak up as best I can." We were in darkness again so it seemed a good time to tell them so I wouldn't se their reactions. "I'm going to be leaving you all tomorrow." There was a moments silence before anyone spoke.

"Man - no way you're gonna leave us!" Haro was an American BMX bike so always spoke like that. As expected, Chopper piped up too.

"But, but you've been here forever dude - even longer than me. Where you goin?" Chopper wasn't American like he pretended he was - he was made in Nottingham.

I paused for a moment because of the realisation that I was going to have to tell them everything. They would know if I was lying.

The decision had been made by Jim and a man called Christopher a couple of weeks previously and I hadn't had the heart to tell all my friends in the lock-up. Jim had collected us over the past forty years and not one of us had ever left - there had been some great stories told; even if we had to listen to the same stories all over again sometimes. Most bicycle memories are short - except for mine, that is. One thing was for certain; none of the others knew what had happened to me when I was young. None of them knew about the adventures I had all those years ago. I think I always felt that it might sound like I was boasting if I told them where I'd been and who with. It's never good to boast.

Ti eventually spoke up. Ti was the quiet seventies racer, also from Nottingham, who'd once been sat on by Joop Zoetemelk for an advertising photograph. He was always rather snooty towards the rest of us and had developed a slightly sardonic air.

"Oh, so have your lugs finally given out - or have they discovered that you're made of more than enough steel to rebuild the Forth Bridge?" He'd been in one of his moods ever since Jim moved him to the front of the garage for someone to look at him a month or so ago. Apparently it was draughty near the door and wasn't good for his decals. I'd never risen to his provocations because I knew that Ti had never been ridden seriously like his brothers; his frame hadn't been true enough for a professional racer. I'd heard Jim tell someone once but I'd never told Ti that I knew.

There was only one bike older than me in the garage and she was in a very sorry state. Jim had dragged Auntie Penny, as we named her, from the top of a hayloft in Essex where she'd been leant against a wall for over a hundred years. She looked sorry because the mice had chewed away most of her solid rubber tyres and her leather saddle was bright green with verdigris. She was also down to a bare pitted metal surface - something she really hated about herself - but she still stood tall and flamingo-like next to us ordinary machines.

"Oh lucky you - I wish I could leave - please tell us, where to? Is it going to be another adventure?"

"I'm not sure that it will be an adventure, Penny. I'm going to a museum."

"You! Why you?" I might have guessed Ti wouldn't be impressed.

"Morris?" Penny always used my name, "I hope you don't mind me asking, but why are you going to a museum? Is there something we don't know about?" She always had intuition about such things - there was clearly something they didn't know but she correctly guessed that it was something that, perhaps, I should have told them about. We were all good friends.

"OK, well this might take some time, but please bear with me. I haven't told anyone about this, ever. You are going be the first to know."

"But if you're going to a museum then someone else must know?" Ti wasn't giving up.

"Shh, you with the skinny little cross bar. Let Morris talk. I might be older than him but we all know he is the wisest in the garage. Morris knows a thing or two. Now listen!" I always liked Auntie Penny.

"Thank you Penny. OK, look, this is not going to be easy and I know I should have told you all before." I paused. "It all started in 1901." I heard a couple of sharp intakes from the assembled bikes, some of whom were, in fact, sadly, disassembled; none of them had guessed that I was that old. "I was one of the last bicycles to be assembled by Mr Morris himself in his shop at 48 the High Street in Oxford. It was just before he got interested in motor-bicycles. He was a proper racing cyclist was Mr Morris, champion of Oxford at one time. Anyway, he went onto better things - they eventually made him Lord Nuffield because he was so good at making cars and selling them. But I digress. So far this isn't much of a story, I know, but it was what happened next that is probably more interesting.

I was bought by a man called Mr Thomas Chapman who called himself Mr Lawrence after his mistress's father - are you with me? In those days you couldn't leave your wife for someone else and simply move in with her without pretending you were married. So that is what they did - and because he was sort of landed gentry - an Irish Baronet, in fact - he had to move frequently so no one recognised him. Anyway, he and his mistress, Sarah, lived in Oxford and they had five sons. He bought me for his son Ned, the second eldest, when he, Ned that is, was around sixteen years old.

Ned was a bit of an odd boy who didn't have many friends, but he did enjoy cycling around the lanes of Oxfordshire with his Father who never seemed to have to go to work. During the summers of 1906 and 1907 he took me on long trips with his one friend, Cyril, to take brass rubbings and look at churches."

"Where is this story going Morris?"

"Bear with me, please, Ti?" I knew it would take a while. "I'm sorry, but this part is quite important. Eventually, young Ned went to Oxford University to study History which, like Archeology, had been a subject dear to his fathers heart. It was there that he hatched his plan to ride me around France to visit Crusaders castles. I think the challenge of riding a bike for such a long way meant as much to him as his need to write something for his studies. Anyway, in July 1908 we set off for the channel ferry and a 3200 mile ride. I don't think he knew it at the time, but the commencement of our trip was just a week or so behind the third running of the famous Tour de France - and we went in roughly the same direction around the country."

"So you went on a long trip - is that it?"

"No, listen - look, I had to tell you those bits so that you would get the background to what happened next." I took another deliberate pause; one which felt quite long in the darkness.

"Morris?" Penny sounded concerned that I hadn't spoken.

"We'd been going for some weeks; Ned was very strong and we were averaging 75 miles a day including the few days when we stopped over for him to write letters to his mother back home. Every day followed a similar pattern; up at 6, large breakfast and on the bike by 6.30. We'd ride through till 1pm and then stop at a castle - he'd worked out his route quite carefully before we'd left. There he would write a little and take photographs before eating again and then pushing on to the next destination where he'd find a cheap hotel - they cost around 2 francs for a room and another 2 francs for the dinner - something he rarely enjoyed because cheap French food didn't suit him.

After a month or so, we'd stopped for the night in a small hamlet called Cuq-Toulsa just north from Carcassonne in the south of France. He'd headed north at this point because he wanted to see a small town called Montgey where, in 1211, a French land owners' soldiers and the local villagers had routed a passing army of 'crusaders'. There was a small plaque to commemorate the event which read 'Ici et aux environs reposent 6000 Croises surpris en embuscade fin d'Avril 1211'. Six thousand, yes, six thousand, mainly German and Frisian crusaders were massacred by the hands of blood thirsty local inhabitants who came out to help the local militia. Even then Ned loved the idea of oppressed people rising up against an evil aggressor who sought the higher moral ground as a reason for invading their domain. Ned spent time walking me round the area of the ancient battle as if picturing the scenes of villagers stoning and clubbing to death the strangely un-armoured and unready foe. None of them survived the onslaught.

The following morning we set out on the dusty N126 heading for Toulouse where Ned had planned a couple of days rest. He was quieter than usual at breakfast and I knew he was still thinking about the events of the previous day. Further up the road we spotted another bicycle. The rider was leant over the bars in a determined fashion; a pair of spare tyres criss-crossed the narrow back and dark woollen shorts - longer than those you'd see a cyclist wearing today - concealing rangy muscular legs that pumped a regular rythm though a fixed wheel racing machine. I felt Ned increase his pace. Ned always liked a challenge.

'Bonjour monsieur!' Ned's French was competent but not very elegant. The reply was in English and slightly curt.

'Good morning to you, sir.' The rider was, to Ned's amazement, a woman. She was a bit older than him, probably in her early 30's, and sported a tough, rugged figure with a dirt-stained face; her cap was stained with sweat and the small goggles perched on the top were dark with dust.

'I'm sorry,' Ned stammered although he didn't explain why he was apologising. 'May we ride together?' It was a strange request as we'd not ridden with anyone else in all the miles we'd covered in France. Perhaps there was something about this athletic woman that intrigued young Ned. She could certainly move her bike well. She nodded with a shrug, and Ned settled alongside her with his hands, like hers, down on the bars - we both had the 'modern' dropped handlebars; I, though, had one of the new three-speed Sturmey-Archer rear hubs which made things a little easier on the hills. She didn't seem to be in the mood to speak, so Ned didn't say anything.

I spoke to the bike - a new Peugeot machine crafted with a Gallic flair that Mr Morris just didn't possess. Even with her dust covered tubes and slightly squeaky chain, she just looked more racy than me.

'Hi!' Bikes don't do languages - we just talk bike. 'How are things - are you going far?' Mme Peugeot looked at me slightly haughtily.

'We're doing the Tour de France.' I couldn't help myself.

'Oh, excuse me, but aren't you a little bit behind the others?...'.

'Non! we started after them because they wouldn't let Marie take part'.

'Oh, why not?'

'Because they only want men in their race.' Oops, seems like I'd ridden across a piece of rocky rue.

'Oh, I am so sorry to hear that. We're doing a sort of Tour de France ourselves - but in a different way. Ned, my rider, is bicycling around France to look at old castles'.

'Well, he's moving at quite a pace - can he keep this up?'

'Oh, yes, he can keep this up all day - he's very strong you know.' I was proud of my Ned.

After a couple of hours at the same breakneck pace, Marie finally spoke.

'I'm stopping for some rest soon. Will you want to be stop with me?' It didn't seem like an easy question for her to ask, but on the basis that Ned had sat, apparently easily, alongside her for many kilometres in the rising heat with a woolen jacket and hat on, she was left with no other choice than to ask him.

'That would be lovely - sorry, miss, what is your name? Mine is Ned.'

"Marie - Marie Marvingt.'

Peugeot and I were propped up against a wall in the shade and Ned and Marie sat opposite each other at a small round wooden table and they talked. And they talked and they talked; they talked about France and the Tour; Marie talked about her unbelievable sporting exploits and her flying.

'I have never thought about flying - what is it like?' Ned was sounding interested. I thought that secretly he didn't actually believe her stories of hunting for seals in the Arctic and swimming through Paris in the Seine - but he didn't show it.

'You have never flown ? Why not? It is so delicious to fly like a bird - the most wonderful thing I have ever done. One day I will fly my own aeroplane. It is the only true freedom.' There was something heroically French in the way she spoke; Ned had met what seemed to him like a real-life Jean d'Arc.

Ned then talked about his interest in the Castles of the Crusades - but this seemed to bore her quite quickly so he adroitly switched to asking where she was from.

'I'm originally from Metz.'

'So, you are a German?'

'No! of course I'm not! No one in Metz is German - they might think we are part of their country, but we are all French, and have always been so.' Ned looked slightly embarrassed. He knew the history of the disputed Alace Lorraine area between France and Germany but didn't know that even after all this time the feeling was still so strong.

'Sorry - I didn't mean to sound rude.'

'You weren't - it's just something we're very sensitive about. Besides I don't live there anymore - since my Father died my family have lived in Nancy.' She was very matter of fact. 'I am surprised you English people aren't a little bit more supportive of us French - surely you must know that Germany is looking to expand and we're likely to be invaded.'

'Do you think so? I'm aware that the British Government has been making moves towards a greater entente with your Prime Minister, Mr Clemenceau - but I fear that he is a little radical for most of them.'

They went on like this for ages. Ned's natural charm and soft demeanor kept things going - he was clearly enjoying her company and she, likewise, seemed intrigued by the determined little man from England who cycled so easily and seemed to know so much about French history.

'So, you say that the French peasants massacred 6,000 Germans just a few miles from here in antiquity? Vive la France! I'm afraid that we, the French people, might have to do so again soon.'

Finally, we set of again on the road to Toulouse - once again Marie set a blistering pace and, again, Ned sat obligingly next to her without threatening the pace but staying resolutely on it. Peugeot was impressed.

'You were right - your rider belies his looks. He is a strong man. But I take it that he hasn't heard of Marie before?'

'No, should he have? I can see she is a great sportswoman, but, no, I don't think he has.'

"Marie Marvingt is a legend in France - she is one of the greatest sports people to have lived - not letting her ride in the Tour is a travesty; such is her prowess, she would beat most of the men in the race.' I doubted this but didn't say anything. 'Mon coureur, Marie, will be world famous one day - I think she could be a saviour of women and even France itself.' Now I decided that sweet little Peugeot had gone a bit too far - but I did like her.

'Well, my rider Ned is also a man that is destined for great things.' I didn't really believe it but I had to counter Peugeot somehow."

"So what happened bud? Did Ned and Marie do great things?" Haro was clearly excited at the prospect.

"Did Marie really save women and all of France?" Penny was old enough to know better but had clearly missed out on a lot with her years in the barn. I could feel a rising enthusiasm in the cold garage. Even Ti was a bit more positive.

"So was this Ned really famous?"

"Oh yes, he became one of the most famous people in the country who was feted wherever he went."

"So what did he do?" I paused again. Not for any other reason than to work out what to say next.

I decided to take them back to the road to Toulouse.

"We rode late into the evening with the large orange sun setting gently in our faces. Ned, tanned from his days in the saddle and Marie with her single minded, single-speed approach to her mission, ploughed on to the City which rose from the flat-lands ahead. Ned liked it when the roads were flat. I think he always felt that wide open spaces suited him better. Many years later after his time in Arabia he spoke about having enjoyed his time in France but having not truly understood the soul of the country. Arabia, he said, was different. The wide open spaces teemed with hidden resources and, as well as dominating the trade routes of the colonial powers of Europe, were ruled by people who loved their country; people who were to be so rudely set upon by the Turks and then let down by the Colonial powers at the Treaty of Versailles after the First World War. Ned, better known by then as Lawrence of Arabia, never got over what he saw as the betrayal of the Arab state he'd fought so hard for.

That night we stayed at a small hotel near the centre of the City. Ned and Marie had dinner in a small café; Peugeot and I were left, nestled together, behind the kitchens. It was warm in Toulouse.

'What do you think will happen tomorrow, Morris?' Peugeot was sleepy after the long day on the road and her bearings sat tight with the grime of the southern French roads. She'd said that Marie would attend to them in the morning with her special lubrication.

'Who knows. Perhaps we'll all be together - or perhaps Ned will want to go a different route to Marie.'

'That would be a shame - it's been nice riding with you today - you have a lovely rouleur who is good for Marie.' As the warmth of the day cooled on the Atlantic breeze, I felt my crossbar touching the still warm steel of the racy little French bike."

"So then what happened dude?" Someone, well, Chopper, was getting impatient.

"Nothing happened - we just waited till the morning - what did you think would happen?"

"Oh Morris, it all sounds so wonderful with Ned and Marie having dinner and you and that saucy little bike together for the night. Did the two of you talk all night?"

"No, I was tired - as I expect Ned was. We all needed sleep."

"Oh, I just thought that, perhaps…no, nothing."

"OK, look, the next day Ned came down at the usual time and we left. I never saw Marie again. I never saw little Peugeot again." I think my voice might have betrayed me a little right at the end.

"I'm sorry Morris - it could have been so very different."

"I have to say that this isn't what I was going to tell you about. I wanted to tell you about the years after the war with Ned when he bought his motorbikes and we settled again in the south of England and he played with the motorboats in the Solent. I was going to tell you about how he died so tragically. I wanted to tell you all so much. But all I've done is told you about the beautiful bike I met in France." There was silence in the garage.

The next day I was taken to a new cycling museum in Oxford and, after being cleaned up, was placed on a stand next another old relic from history.

Her name, it turned out, was Peugeot. We were to be together again; this time Ned couldn't ride me away.

Missoula Mission (1897)

"Hey buddy, you boys been far?"

"Yeah…a long way fella. Longer than any of us thought was possible. We just been ridden all the way from Fort Missoula, Montana."

"Montana?"

"Yessir, 1900 hundred miles in 41 days - we're all here too. The Lord only knows how, but every last one of us present - all 23 bikes - completed the ride."

"I was wonderin' why the 10,000 St Louis folks turned out so eagerly to watch you parade today - so why the ride?"

"Long story man. But one that will go down in the history of bicycling; the greatest ride ever - and completed by the Buffalo soldiers of the 25th Infantry Cycling Corps."

"I ain't never heard of the Cycling Corps. So you're with the US Army then?"

"Yep, sure are, and one day we'll be famous for what we just done."

"You must be pretty tired then?"

"I guess so, but not that tired that I can't tell you what happened; listen up, someone needs to hear what really happened on that journey. Mark my words, 'cos it'll all be changed by the time the Press get to hear of it and that darned journalist writes it the way he wants."

"What d'you mean?"

"Well, a white guy call Boos came along with us for the ride 'cos the two white officers wanted to prove that the bicycle was best suited as a transportation device for troops by testing it 'most thoroughly' - and yes, we showed that a bicycle corps could travel twice as fast as cavalry and infantry for less than a third of the cost across all sorts of terrain - and we don't need feedin' nor restin' like horses! But it wasn't all that simple and whilst they're admitting to a few flats and a couple of frame breaks, they haven't talked to anyone about what really happened out there. "

"What do you mean?"

"Look, you'll see we're not like usual bikes. We were built specifically for the US Army by A G Spalding in Massachusetts - you know, the worlds biggest bicycle manufacturer? Take a look and at our stainless steel wheel rims, tandem spokes for extra strength, extra strong forks and crowns, luggage carriers and brakes; we even got Christy saddles. Without equipment we weigh nearly 35 pounds - and then we can carry another 25 pounds of equipment including, a knapsack, a blanket roll, a shelter and even a rifle with fifty rounds of ammunition. And, you know what, those tough men who rode us here went through every privation and suffering imaginable on that trip."

"So what happened?"

"Well it was rough from the very start of the journey - we had snow and hail and rain for the first ten days - man, that was hard and would have been enough to have broken most men. The poor boys only had two sets of clothes so nothin' was ever dry. But then we reached Nebraska and it got hot - so hot our frames stung the hand to touch and the riders was getting blisters from the bars. But it started to go real wrong in the town of Alliance. Moss, the Lieutenant leading us got ill from poisonous water - well most of the men got a little ill, but he had to stay behind to convalesce. That meant the Doctor was put in charge and we then spent five gruesome days crossing the Nebraska Sandhills - I never seen such a test of man and machine; day after day of just sand, sun and cactus - they got swollen tongues and burned skin and the like, an' we got sand in our bearin's and prickly pear bush spines in our tyres. Well, it was a test for all of 'em except, apparently, Corporal Eugene Jones; he didn't seem to be taken ill like the rest of them. But then he started to make trouble with the doctor. Jones had been trouble since the start but Moss and the Sergeant, Mingo Saunders, knew how to control him. With Moss gone and Saunders out of sorts, Jones started to badger the doc."

"What did Jones want?"

"He wanted out - he'd had enough of the sufferin' - but the doctor wouldn't let 'im leave for the nearby railroad station. Then Jones said he would expose the doctor as a fraud - somehow he knew that the doctor had failed his final examinations and was in the Army under a false pretence. So they did a deal and agreed that Jones would leave the trip when they reached the town of Grand Island - the doctor would say that he had an injury. None of the others knew 'bout deal - but we bikes knew - we overheard 'em talking."

"So then what happened?"

"Well, when we got to Grand Island, Lieutenant Cook re-joined us and the doctor told Jones that he was OK to leave. As the Corporal left the hotel early the next morning to catch a train, the doctor followed him and shot him dead alongside the railroad."

"How do you know he shot him?"

"Because he rode on me to catch up with Jones - he just rode up behind him as he swaggered up the sidewalk towards the station and shot him in the back with his revolver. It was early and there no one about. We then went back to the Hotel and he told Cook that he had let Jones go because he was sick. Nothing more was said."

"So he killed him in cold blood!"

"Yep - an' we rode out of town straight after breakfast and continued on our journey. Never heard another word about Jones. I guess the townsfolk thought he must have been shot because he was black; they say it isn't unusual in Nebraska."

"So what now? - what you guys going to do now?"

"I dunno - I would like to think that the whole world knows what we've done and everything will be different - we should be famous!"

"I wouldn't count on it."

"What?"

"Well I guess you haven't heard what happened earlier this month whilst you were toiling across the sand? Two steamships, the Excelsior and the Portland arrived in San Francisco bringing in prospectors from the Yukon with $2 Million of gold in their bags - there is only one story in the Press at the moment - and it ain't you guys. There's a gold rush goin' on!"

Superseded

3rd October 2010

It's been three weeks. This isn't easy; I still don't understand why I am here or what I did wrong. The door has been locked shut every day since I was incarcerated; all I can do is look out of the small window at the grass and watch the little birds flitting in and out of the trees. Louis came in once, but only briefly, to check that was I was still where I'd been left - I don't know where he thought I'd be going as I was still clamped to his metal contraption holding me upright, preventing me moving. Louis didn't use me like he'd said he would when he first brought me to this god-forsaken place; he just stared coldly at me. Looking back, I think my first day here was the strangest ever; all the things I was used to doing had stopped; needlessly bound to a hard concrete floor with a single, stained window and locked-tight door, I wanted the rumble of the road 'neath my frame, scared I'd been sidelined, retired, made lame.

6th October 2010

Louis came to see me after work last night. I think I must have been lost in some forgotten dream as I looked, unseeing, into the darkness of the window panes; the sun sets early now and there is virtually nothing of the evening for me to look out on; the birds are silent. The sound of the key in the lock and the door being wrenched open caught me by surprise; the blast of cold air, followed by the click of the light switch- I jumped in my shackle. 'I'm going to be using you soon' was all he said, but with a slightly ominous tone. The he set up a lap-top on the bench, found the wifi, and set about downloading some software. I watched intently with my chain held tight, but I couldn't quite see what he was doing. He even sat on me briefly as he adjusted the screen. For a moment I thought I was going be used like before, but I realised that he wasn't properly dressed for that. When we did 'that' he always got dressed up. Besides, it was late, and we never went out in the dark.

7th October 2010

I've waited all day for him to come. I didn't like the way he'd treated me in the months before he locked me up in here, but now I am just looking for any sort of contact from him; however rough and abusive he'd been in the past, I just want to be with him again. We'd been through a lot over the years and it hadn't been all bad; I still loved him.

I think it was his new job that had made him so angry. We've achieved so much together, but then he started the new job and he used me less and less; we stopped going out during the week because he was too tired from work and at weekends there was always more work to be done on the house, the car, the garden. I think I just got forgotten.

Then there was his weight; only 76 kilos when he started the new job, but within months he was piling on the pounds; I think he was also drinking more than before. That's when he started to get rough with me when we were together. It was as if it was my fault that he couldn't perform anymore - every time he went for the finish, the climax of the piece, he failed. I tried to help as much as I could, but he just got worse. Shortly after, we endured that disastrous overseas trip with the other guys; it was there that he found his new love and I was put away.

She was from Italy and, yes, she was younger and prettier than me - a model that other men would envy him for. I only saw them together a couple of times, but I knew that he was completely taken.

10th October 2010

He finally came in to see me this evening, and was dressed for action. After fiddling with his computer for a bit, he mounted me and began to turn the pedals. It wasn't good - within only a minute or two of spinning and heaving, he'd built up a horrible sweat and panted and wheezed like your worst drunken lover. Any finesse or touching words were gone. Just brutish expletives and angry attempts at speed with the machine he used to love and caress. It wasn't long before he stormed out into the darkness, slamming the door as he left. I sat there in the dark with his lager-laced sweat still dripping on my bars. The light was slammed off in his hasty exit, but the computer screen rudely glared the truth of his failure. There, in numbers, were the results of his seven minutes twenty two seconds of physical collapse. Max Heart rate - 189. Max speed - 42 Kms. Max power - 240 watts. He'd never been so weak.

17th October 2010

This is abuse. I can't take this much more. Louis hates me. This evening he called me a 'useless pile of shit'. I don't know what to do. At some point I think he's just going to smash my crossbar. He never blames this evil contraption that he has tethered me to or himself for his pathetic performances. It's all my fault. I'm old, and ugly, and worthless. His wretched computer seems to be telling him that I'm the reason he's rubbish. I even saw what his friends were saying to him on the screen - he moved me closer so that he could read them during a session. One of them, his new coach, Alex, even asked what sort of old bike he was riding - apparently he could see me with the online streaming of Louis's workout. I've never felt so low. Tonight I felt my bearings contract a little as the first frost of winter seeped under the door. My bright red frame is dimming with age and the tiny chips and scratches that have been collected over the years are darkening and looking more pronounced. I'm tired of it all.

29nd October 2010

Like yesterday, and the day before, and the day before that, Louis came to me again this evening. Things are starting to get a little better. The numbers are starting to improve and I can feel his rhythm coming back. I'm not labouring so much at the lugs; my dropouts less distressed, my bottom bracket less bothered; the work is less wretched. He even smiled when he'd finished with me; his beer infused ballast is beginning to melt away as the time spent burning calories means less at the bar. Things are changing.

The constantly changing numbers on the screen confused me at first; previously we'd spent more time on the road where everyone knew the best work was done. But Alex wanted numbers; Alex could only work with numbers. Alex didn't ride a bike and only knew how to coach by numbers. Alex wasn't a person - he was a 'virtual' coach who did everything for Louis except, well, coach. The training plans were expensive and the one-to-one's using real-time Facetime were paid by the quarter hour. Alex had coached some of the best. He was worth it. Louis was now earning a lot more with the new job so he was worth it too. Nowadays, he said, everyone has a coach.

December 5th 2010

He brought her in this evening. I steeled myself - as only I could - whilst he leant her gently against the wall; she stared at me with the dull demeanor that only carbon can. 'Can't you speak?' I asked. She shrugged her stem and looked down at her neat little pedals. 'Well?' I knew she was too embarrassed to engage with an ugly old bike like me. It wasn't her that was making Louis strong again. She was just for him to look at, to dream about, to pretend he was a 'pro'. I was the real deal. I would make him a winner again. He knew that I was the one that had made him good all those years before. She was just a pretty thing with carbon this and carbon that and electronic these and calibrated those; she couldn't make him go faster with the sexy sweeping curves of her rear stays or the gently tapered tube of her steerer. Only I could make him go faster. I was the one he loved. I was the one that loved him. She never did speak to me. I guess her being Italian didn't help.

January 23rd 2011

We're now moving on beautifully. Our workouts in the garage are beginning to show results. I think he's starting to realise that I am the only bike for him. The numbers are good - we're doing full mountain stages three times a week, interspersed with functional threshold sessions and a close adherence to the latest online regime posted by Alex. The training Stress Scores are adhered to like they were the bible and intensity factors and variability index's are calculated to ensure that he's on target for all the racing he's planning on doing in the coming season. Well, that is what he wrote to his online friends. He is certainly putting the time in. Best of all, he's loving me like he did before; the touch of his hands on my hoods and the reassuring feel of the pressure from his feet make me shiver beneath him. I can't wait for the sunshine. I can't wait for us to get out back on the road.

April 24th 2011

It's less than a week before his first race of the season - tonight he came in and did some quick hard repeats - he maxed out at 400 watts for two bursts. Quite an improvement from the dark days of October; I think I'm beginning to understand the numbers on the computer - we didn't do them in the old days. I also can't wait see what wheels he's got for me - my old Mavics have certainly seen better days. He's going to have to clean me up of course; I've got a lot of stains on my frame and my brake blocks need replacing - for tyres, I thought that the new Vittoria Graphenes sounded about right for me - plenty of grip and a long lasting tread that should last the season. That sounds like me; the stayer; the faithful speedster with the slim elegant lines. Come on, bring it on! Let's race!

April 25th 2011

Something strange happened this evening. Louis came in with her again and spent at least an hour with her clamped high in the blue stand. He lightly lubricated all her bearings, and, with a super soft cloth, gently rubbed her thick green tubes to an even more lustrous shine. Her deep dark carbon rims sat stealthily on their spokes - they never smiled, nor gave away any other emotion; they just sat there like miserable black holes against the empty garage wall. Dull, despicable weaponry. She was a machine so bereft of emotion and character that even the lubricants didn't ease her demeanour.

Oddly, Louis didn't speak or even look at me as he attended to her. After all those weeks of increasing intensity together, he was now acting like a man confronted with the ex-wife and his lover; I might as well have not been there. Was he embarrassed by me? When he left that evening he took her with him into the house. I knew that's where they went because after he locked the door on me I could hear her spanking new Vittoria's squealing on the parquet in the hallway - I could even tell that she was left at the bottom of his stairs where I used to sit. He's been using me.

May 2nd 2011

He raced today. He didn't win. I knew he hadn't won because he brought her into the garage and threw her against the wall. 'You useless piece of rubbish!' was all he said. I didn't know what to do. Well, it was never going to be much as I was still clamped into the trainer. But, then, to my huge surprise, he went over to her, angrily ripped her wheels away from her, and turned to face me with a wheel in each hand. He smiled. 'OK, let's give it a go - Sunday; it's you and me again. You ready?' Of course I was ready.

Double Dutch

We have lived with the Norton family for a very long time; none of them really knew how we got here, until recently. The truth turned out to be more than just a surprise.

The popular notion, often repeated by Auntie Clare in her 'Granny told me, so it must be true' way, was that the two of us were ridden to the house in the village of Blakeney, Norfolk , by Dutch cousins in the 1930's; the story goes that they were on a touring holiday from Amsterdam and popped in to see Grandfather Daniel and Grandmother Winnie. Whilst this sounded conceivable, it didn't explain how the 'cousins' might have returned home again without us - and why, for that matter, the family don't appear to have Dutch cousins anymore? Whatever, the story wasn't true. That is not how we became part of the Norton family home.

Daniel Norton was Auntie Clare's grandfather and the husband of Winnie who, we suppose, told Clare the story of the Dutch cousins when she was younger. But the two of us knew that Daniel and Winnie didn't always tell the truth.

In the late summer of 1939, us two bicycles, made by the great Dutch bike builders, Fongers, were taken quite unexpectedly from our home at the Het Loo Palace, to the City of Den Helder at the very northern tip of the Netherlands. Yes, we belonged to and were frequently ridden around the grounds of the Palace by the Queen, Wilhelmina, and her daughter Juliana during their stays at the Royal summer residence. No one told us what was happening on that last day of August, but we were taken to the bustling Naval yard and placed on the open deck of a small coastal fishing boat. With us was a small crew of three Royal Dutch Navy personnel, and two of the Queens staff; Henrik Steward, the most obscure and guarded of her secretaries, and a pretty young woman that we didn't recognise; the two of them went straight down to the small crew quarters below decks. The boat slipped her moorings late that night and we chugged out of the harbour to the open water. It was calm and pleasant; behind us the lights of the city slowly disappeared into the flat waters of the southern North Sea as the skipper set a course due west into the darkness.

Hours later, when the sun began to make the grey sea blue again, it seemed our journey was coming to an end; the crew started to scan ahead where a low coastline could be seen and, after a bit of discussion, seemed to agree on a long sandy beach facing north as a place to head for. It transpired that this was the north coast of Norfolk in England - although why we being sent here, we had no idea; the Queen herself didn't have much time for the English although she had apparently liked Queen Victoria when they met years previously. It was said her dislike was because of what been done in the Transvaal and the Orange Free State after the Boer Wars. Also, the British upper class politeness is not appreciated by the Dutch; we find it rather insincere and hypocritical. But that's just us.

It was no secret that Hitler's Germany were looking like they might want to take over the world again and we knew that our Queen had been in various discussions about what would happen if the Netherlands was overrun - but was she really thinking of going to England?

It is fair to say that we didn't know anything about boats or the sea, but where we were headed didn't look like a place where this sort of boat would be able to land.....the waves were breaking onto the empty beach. Eventually it became clear when we rounded a sandy headland and slipped into a previously unseen harbour where the waters were calmer; a small coastal village came into view across the marshes. When we finally arrived, the two staff with their bags, and the two of us, were simply dropped onto the sunny quayside and our fishing boat turned around and headed straight back out to sea. There were no good-byes and the boat didn't even tie-up. We were just left there.

Immediately across the road was a smart pebble and brick building with the words 'The Blakeney Hotel' written on a squeaky sign swinging in the gentle breeze on the front wall. Hendrik and the young woman, Margrit, went into the building and left us against the front wall under the sign. The place was tranquil enough and the people walking about seemed, well, almost Dutch. After a short while a young, smartly dressed English couple walked along the road towards us.

"Look, Winnie, dearest!" The man started to say, "look, at the two bicycles outside the hotel - they're here. Our guests are here. Come on, quickly, they must be exhausted." Five minutes later we were being pushed up the hill with the English couple leading the way to a fine English house near the church.

The next thing we knew was that we were to be staying at the house for a few days - I think the plan was we would be ridden to a place called Cromer, some 20kms along the coast, to catch a train that would eventually take us somewhere just north of London where Hendrik and the woman had some business to attend to. But something went wrong. In fact, two dreadful things occurred that meant that we were never to leave Blakeney.

Firstly, the second World War began with Adolf Hitler's Nazi Germany invading Poland on the 1st of September, then Britain and France declared war two days later. Daniel Norton was one of the few people in Blakeney to have a telephone in his house and he spent over an hour on the afternoon of the 3rd talking urgently to someone. It turned out that the Netherlands had, as expected, declared themselves neutral in the conflict, but it meant that our being in Britain was now an altogether different proposition. Daniel announced that we weren't to leave the house for any reason. We were effectively under house arrest with people who were supposed to be helping us.

The second dreadful thing to happen occurred at the end of the first week, when Daniel had been drinking whisky in the garden all afternoon with Hendrik - who had grown increasingly uneasy at his and Margrit's plight as the days passed. Us two bikes were, once again, leant against a wall and had been watching them both. Suddenly they started to argue. I only heard a few words, but I could hear that it was something to do with the English King George. Hendrik had obviously said something that had incensed Daniel and he'd started to get very angry indeed; stood, with his hands in his pockets, and shouting at the still seated Hendrik who appeared pinched but unperturbed, the furious tirade went on for over a minute. Now Dutch people are known for their reserved nature, but there must have been something said by Daniel that eventually riled even the usually unflappable Hendrik. He suddenly stood up and slapped Daniel across the face. Daniel staggered back before gathering himself and launching a fearful attack on his assailant. Hendrik fell to the ground from a punch that knocked him cold and, as he landed, his head struck a row of tilted bricks that marked the edge of the pavement. He didn't move. The two ladies came quickly from the house.

" Daniel, what just happened?" There was genuine panic in Winnie's voice.

"He….he tripped - we were arguing and he just tripped on the stones - I think he banged his head." Hendrik hadn't moved since he fell.

"I think he's dead." Margrit's words bore a horrible finality. A tear rolled down her cheek as, kneeling beside him, she held her lover's hand. Winnie knelt down too and put her arm around Margrit. A strange silence fell on the sunny walled garden.

The truth was buried there in the garden. Winnie and Daniel decided that evening that the young Margrit, who it transpired was simply Henrik's lover and nothing to do with his mission to request the King of England's help to rescue his Queen in the event of an imminent invasion by the Germans, had to go too. They couldn't have her in the house if their country was at war - besides, how would they explain the death of Hendrik? They'd only agreed to help the couple's secret assignment on the request of a City colleague of Daniels at Rothschilds Bank in London. Daniel and Winnie agreed on a pact and told the relevant authorities that the two Dutch people had unexpectedly left in the middle of the night without a word. The story of the 'cousins' was coined. Besides, there was a war on so it was not as if anyone would be looking for them.

Seventy-five years later, in the late summer of 2014, when the house was still being used as a summer residence by the Norton family, and we were still in regular use for rides to the shops, Daniel's son, Robert, was granted planning permission to build an extension to the rear of the house and over part of the walled garden. Some of the family, Auntie Clare in particular, objected to digging up of Grandpa's 'favourite' lawn where their children played every summer; but Robert was insistent. At the beginning of the Autumn term when all the children had gone back to school and family back to their jobs in the City, the diggers moved in. On the second day of ground working they found the remains of Hendrik and Margit lying together with their bags just four feet below the surface of the beautiful lawn. We'd know they were there all the time because we'd seen them buried. It was been a secret that we couldn't have told even if we'd wanted.

Tube Love

I have been very lucky; I have been loved by two people. In the thirty seven years since I was built by Mike - I was frame number 212 - there have been only six months that I wasn't loved - my first owner hardly rode me at all during that time because I think I was too big for him; so he doesn't count.

I guess you may be thinking that me, a slightly scruffy thirty-seven year old with replacement parts from all eras and cycling disciplines, must be slightly bonkers to even consider that I might have been 'loved'. I know, it sounds completely ridiculous. But please, listen carefully to what I'm going to tell you.

Mike, my builder, wasn't well in 1978 when he put me together. Mike was dying of incurable cancer and he knew it. Mike, in human terms, was also alone; an only child, he never had a wife or children and his parents were dead. Mike had devoted his life to building perfect bicycle frames; racing bicycle frames. Not just perfectly true and perfectly strong, but frames built with an attention to detail that verged on the obsessive. It would take him months to build a bike; weeks of filing, and sanding and grinding to obtain perfectly sleek and gorgeously mitred double butted Reynolds tubes - before meticulously brazing them with brass to bond the triangles together to the exacting requirements of his customers. I was Mike's last frame and, due to his illness, I took longer to be built than those before me; by the end there was virtually no strength in his hands. Late one night at the workshop, Mike spoke to me quietly in his soft Berkshire burr as he caressed my powder-coated tubes; his hands shook a little as he carefully applied the decal bearing his name to my head tube. That is the time when a bicycle becomes something; the moment when we become more than the sum of our parts. The moment I was born.

"Go my beauty - go and conquer the world - you're a special bike and I've given you everything I have. I want you to be enjoyed and cherished as much as I have enjoyed making you. If no other frame I have made is remembered, I just want you to be my star." He sat with me in his warm, craftsman's hands as the rain fell heavily on the skylight above us. I was born in a storm.

After my brief time with owner number one, the early days with my second owner weren't that promising either; there was the disqualification from a local time trial event because one of the organisers had seen my young owner riding his other bike whilst pushing me alongside in a bid to get to the event without actually riding on my delicate tubular tyres....they were always likely to puncture. The official said it 'was the most foolish thing he'd ever seen!' and sent us all home. Then there was the early morning fall during another time trial when the same young man lost concentration in the fog and rode too close the kerb - guaranteed to result in a messy outcome. Finally, there was the unseemly retirement when my (still) young rider thought he might be able to stay with a certain Mr Sean Yates of Tour de France and Peugeot fame who'd overtaken him at the start of a 100k pro-am time trial event; we ended up in a field with bent (thankfully borrowed) wheels and a bruised bottom. Sean, incidentally, carried on to break the course record. Despite the spills, there was some sort of progression and even the chance that my rider might have joined a top club with prospects. Somehow this all eluded him. But the bond was there - I'd been his biggest ever purchase and whether it was combination of his guilt at my expense or his actual talent, we did get to do some pretty good rides.

As can happen with youngsters, he succumbed to the usual human vices; drinking, smoking and screwing were his favourites; all of which, when not moderated, can only be detrimental to a riding career. Many years later, after his ultimate divorce and re-birth as a cyclist with potential, he started to take me seriously once again; I think I was the love he didn't realise he'd had all the time he'd been giving everything else a try - most of our time apart I'd spent waiting quietly in the garden shed and had to be content with just the occasional wistful look and apologetic words.

Things changed; he changed; my wheels and my forks and my brakes and gears changed. Everything changed. He bought other bikes for other rides - even a tandem for his other love, and he started to take cycling seriously again. We began to spend more time together and we started to move properly again, together. I was becoming a contender for every ride - he even thought to time trial me again - after nearly forty years!

Then, one day, out of the blue, he felt that I was the bike he needed to ride for the National 24 hour Time Trial. Surely, no one in their right mind would ride a forty year old frame in an event that is only ever won by superior technology or physiology - and usually a combination of the two? He wasn't Bradley; I wasn't carbon; he wasn't Lance; I wasn't aero; my wheels were aluminium for goodness sake; I even had stainless steel Campagnolo cable clamps on my top tube! OK, so he put a few time trial necessities on me and borrowed a set of better wheels - but, surely, I was still far too old. Was I just going to be an excuse for not doing well?

The result couldn't have been foreseen by anyone - OK, so in the past, through dogged determination, he'd made the top five a couple of times and a podium once, but win it? No one ever thought that was going to happen. As it was, the event was mired by a huge Atlantic thunderstorm that washed across the course with hurricane force winds and a deluge of biblical proportions; the Shimano Di2 electronic gear changers were shorting and the BB30 bottom brackets sucking up the debris before belching out their bearings; the finely exfoliated athletes in skin-suits and booties succumbed to the cold. We won with the lowest winning mileage for thirty years. We won because I was old and wise and he never gave up on me. He talked to me through the darkness and turmoil of the night; I soothed his soreness and steered him through the storm. I was born in a storm, remember?

I'm blessed because I've been loved. Thank you Mike, and thank you John.

Solitary

I'm all about rhythm and balancing skills,

The best at me prosper by perfecting the drills;

Drills that teach them to look dead ahead,

By pushing my pedals, not coasting instead.

I'm odd for a bike as you'll soon find out,

And my history is mired with jokes and doubt;

A conveyance so singularly simple as I

Can only raise questions like how, and why?

But I do have a purpose and a grand manifesto;

One wheel is plenty for those in the know!

Two wheels are easy when attached to a frame;

But I need practice for proficiency and fame.

When finally mastered I can stop on the dots

Or speed along roads at a fair rate of knots.

Alas, my story's not all smiles and fun,

My first thirty years were pretty humdrum;

Beginning in Barnsley at the back of a shop,

An afternoon's doodle; a bicycle chop.

Sold to a troupe of miserable freaks,

They worked in a big-top, white faces, red cheeks.

His made-up frown was designed to clown the kids all around the ring.

But they all looked to mumsy when he fell, awkward, clumsy,

To the sawdust, in a well-rehearsed sting.

He was the clown whose living I was making,

Falling was part of our twice daily faking;

But clowns aren't that funny and tricks aren't that clever

When, after years of performing, every day becomes, 'whatever'.

I toured with the circus for many a year

Was ridden by clowns from High Wycombe to Highclere.

They none of them loved me nor treated me well;

Just rode me in circles; their living; my hell.

I should be more grateful at my travelling lot,

But it's not like he was famous like Miss Laura Trott!

Bright coloured silks and a face of surprise,

Made Clarence the clown the target of pies.

Custard, of course, was in all of the jokes,

But not much fun when it's caught in your spokes.

Chased by fools with flippers for feet,

Backfiring cars with an ejector seat,

To entertain kids was our singular purpose,

But every day made me more want to purchase

A ticket to Ryde or wherever I could

Be loved and ridden for ever, for good.

One wheel, not two, was all I was given,

Designed by a dreamer who thought steered could be driven.

Gears are for girls, brakes for the bonkers

Unicycles were made for men with conkers!

Always moving means never stood still,

Just like the circus; a perpetual treadmill.

All around the country, chasing the dough,

Stuck in a jam on a journey of woe.

The clowns who learned on me swore quite a lot

Unicycles take more time than they've got.

Gin was their pleasure away from the ring;

Faces of joy turned ugly to sing.

Songs that were bawdy and crude about cupid,

Songs that said children were worthless and stupid.

They didn't realise that with children came mums;

Who paid for the tickets to fill seats with bums.

When big tops were loaded the owners got flash,

Clowns were sent home with pockets of cash.

Cash to burn on whatever they'd like;

More make-up, more gin, more custard, new bike?

Escaping was never an option for me,

'Cos one wheel can't turn without balance and he;

Clarence's balance was legendary good;

Backwards or forwards he rode like he should.

So alone I couldn't leave that dusty old ring;

What would become of this lonely, one-wheeled thing?

The elephants were nevertheless sadder than me,

They could remember their lives when free.

The toothless lion gave a pitiful roar,

Horses got giddy, monkeys got sore;

Stung by the whip to jump for the trainers,

The circus made hay for owners and campaigners.

I befriended a mouse who travelled along,

John, his name, small, brave and strong.

'Always believe there's a much better way,

The worlds much bigger than a stage ringed with hay.'

Day after day I repeated his line

And one day was rewarded with news of a sign;

The circus was closing, we were all for the chop,

Soon I'd be free from working the top.

Free from the top-hat that called himself Master,

Free from being a by-word for laughter.

If it wasn't for anti's making circuses stop,

The elephants and lions would still work till they drop.

As the clowns and the high-wire wasn't frightening enough,

They all took a severance and told, 'get out! Tough!

A tent's not the place for your sort of fun,

Go join the Canadians and run rings round the sun.'

Sold at auction for a song and some money;

Entertainer, his profession, name of Sonny.

A new coat of red paint - yes, very daring!

A much needed service restored my old bearing.

We now ply our trade amongst tourists and shoppers

Whilst keeping an eye out for tall mean coppers;

They don't like our sort on the Capital's streets,

So move us along to neighbouring beats.

But people still throng along to the square

To stand, and clap, and cheer, and stare.

But instead of being a figure of fun,

I'm now treated equally, fairly, we're one.

One wheel, one act, one purpose, one direction,

Sonny and I are uni-cycling perfection.

The one-wheeled bike will be here for good, but remember, we'll always be misunderstood.

Faithfully Yours

"So what's the deal then love?"

"What do you mean?"

"Come on - you don't look like the rest of us, do you." I was being a bit harsh but the machine hung next to me in the shed did look particularly odd - even though there was something about her that was purposeful and strong. She'd seemed to me to be sulking when they first brought her in - as if she wasn't expecting to be put away.

"No I'm not like you all - I'm from Scotland." She wasn't exactly warming up but at least she was talking.

"I don't mean that - we know where you're from - I mean, well, you're just made differently to everyone else here." There was a short silence. I guess she was looking around at the rest of us standard track bikes hung by our saddles in the darkened store room under the track.

"Yes, well, I was made in the kitchen wasn't I." Now I knew some bike builders were a bit strange but I didn't know of any that made bikes in the kitchen. "Graeme, my rider, made me all by himself in the kitchen - and he told me that I have got a soul; he even named - Old Faithful." There was a wistfulness in her voice. I didn't know what soul was any more than I knew any bikes that could name the actual person that had built them. I was made by some young apprendista at a frame builders shop in Torino, Italy. And while I got the frame builders name put on my tubes it was the scruffy lad with poor workshop skills that did all the work. He was the reason my lugs are so uneven...and why I ended up at this crappy bike track in Norway.

"So why did he make you look like that?"

"Like what?"

"Like you're missing a crossbar and most of your handlebars?"

"I Dunno - but it makes us go fast."

"And what about your bottom bracket - is that some new Shimano unit?" Where I came from everyone had Campagnolo parts.

"No, he made it from the bearings of an old Hotpoint washing machine."

By this point, as you can imagine, I was really starting to wonder what was going on. The bike next to me had been rushed into the store that afternoon before her rider had attempted and then failed to break the world hour record on the track above us. And he'd done it on another slightly less funny-looking bike - well, what was he thinking? You don't just turn up virtually unannounced and beat a world record.

"OK, so why, Old Faithful, have you been put down in here with us?"

"Well, Graeme and me are going to break the hour record tomorrow morning."

"Really? Tomorrow? Do you know what that means? That record has stood since '84 - it is held by the legendary Francesco Moser - you know, Lo sceriffo?" The sad-looking bike with its odd white frame was seeming slightly deluded to me; perhaps she was only as mad as her rider - nobody, not even Moser had ever been crazy enough to attempt the hour record two days running.

"So? Graeme says that records are meant to be broken - he said that he's as good as broken it already."

"But didn't 'Graeme' just fail in his attempt on the record this evening?"

"Yes, but he was on that other bike - the one that 'they' made him ride. Me and him broke the Scottish 10 mile record together recently after he'd been drunk the night before - so now he's going to do the hour, tomorrow morning, with me - and not with that other bike!"

"Really."

[Scot, Graeme Obree, set about Francesco Moser's long standing world record on 16 July 1993, at the Vikingskipet Velodrome in Norway. He missed the record by nearly a kilometre but decided to go back again the

next day to try again on his favourite bike, Old Faithful; he duly beat the World record by 445 metres.]

Time Traveller

Mike clipped his pedals in and I felt the starters hand tighten on my seat post. He always gets tense now and never speaks to timekeepers; He just focuses ahead as our minute man disappears up the road. Mike likes this course. The dual carriageway start means that competitors rarely lose sight of the rider in front and Mike expects us to catch them well before the roundabout which arrives at around nine minutes thirty into the time trial - well, it does for someone as quick as Mike.

"20 seconds!"

Mike slides forwards and prepares to rise up from his saddle so that he's in perfect position to explode away from the start; four deep breaths to pre-oxygenate his eight and a half litre lungs are taken; preparation for the first minute of all-out effort that can leave him seeing double before his heart rate catches up and pumps enough blood to his brain. I feel the tension build as the pressure rises on the left pedal - Mike always pushes off with his left.

"10 seconds, nine, eight," Mike's hand momentarily leaves the low set bar to press the start on his timer. "five, four, three, two, one, go!" The stresses are huge as his muscular body leans forward and pours five hundred watts of raw power through the pedal. Once again, I feel my bottom bracket squeeze gently away from the arc of the pedal arm, my handlebar stem creak mournfully under the upward pressure and the chain hiss against the teeth on the huge carbon chain wheel. We're off.

"Go Mike - have a good one, Mike" The encouraging words are barely heard through the slow acceleration away from the line - the gear is very big; matched only by Mikes thighs. The cadence will always be low with Mike; he's a power man that excels in the flat 10's. Ten miles of all out savage power; lungs grasping for air, lactic cursing through veins and tyres clinging precariously to the asphalt; ten miles, usually under eighteen minutes.

The weekly Farnham Road Club tens run every Wednesday evening through the season on the H10/8 course on the A31. Mike Jarvis isn't a member but we go every Wednesday nevertheless. Every Wednesday Mike Jarvis wins. On that particular day we arrived as usual at the quiet stretch of road where everyone parks up for the event; Mike set me up on the turbo for his obligatory thirty-minute warm up. He always uses the trainer so as not to run the risk of a puncture in one of the lightweight Vittoria tubulars that shroud the Zipp carbon wheels.

Five minutes into our warm-up we were disturbed.

"Hey, are you Mike Jarvis?" He looked up, almost accusingly from his Garmin monitor, and stared at the diminutive young woman stood with her bike in front of him - it was dark carbon with deep-section wheels, but no branding. No one ever spoke to Mike when he warmed up. He mumbled a begrudging affirmative and looked back down at the monitor. "OK - nice to meet you." He didn't even flinch at the faintly sarcastic comment and, mercifully, she wandered off and left us alone.

His minute man was, in fact, that small girl. We'd never seen her before and he kept us away from the start until she'd begun her ride. As a rule Mike didn't talk to anyone if he could help it, and he certainly wasn't going to talk with some random chatty girl just before the off.

We got up to race speed after only a hundred metres and Mike's regular rasping breaths could be clearly heard above the noise of the booming 808 rear disc wheel as we crashed across an uneven section of tarmac. Soon after we'd suffer the regular transverse cracks running across the road every twenty metres for a mile or so through the fast Froyle section. The effect on the bike speed and a riders resolve can be severely hampered by the ensuing bumps, but Mike knows to drive on through them; the smooth section after is always better when we hit it at speed and are able to exert maximum loading for the slight down-slope that follows. This was where we would expect to start to close in on the rider ahead. Strangely, we didn't. There was no sign of the girl; had she punctured or had a mechanical and slipped back to Control unseen? I knew Mike was perturbed and I could see him starting to glance across at the riders on the other side of the road on the return leg to the finish. He was distracted.

"What the f...?" There she was; head down, long legs spinning, and in a perfect aero position. She'd passed her own minuteman and was closing in on the next rider. I felt the surge of watts as Mike put his own head down again and flicked through the readings on the Garmin. We were on track for a good time but it wasn't enough for Mike.

After taking the Hollybourne roundabout faster than we'd ever done with my right hand pedal getting within millimetres of grounding, we headed back up the A31 towards Farnham. The chase was on. I worked out that the girl was quicker than us at the halfway point - we were forty seconds from the middle of the roundabout when we crossed - and Mike was now doing everything to re-take her. We passed the two minute man in a blur, and, shortly after that, the three minute man. Mike was churning the 55/11 gear with everything he had. As we closed in on the final half mile, our speed topped thirty four miles an hour; a rising panic pulsed through the bike as Mike's breathing reached feverish levels and the sweat dripped incessantly from his helmet; we were starting to sway from side to side. The last hundred yards and still no sign of the girl. Surely we'd done enough.

The screen read seventeen minutes eleven seconds and was not just a big PB, but was also good enough for the course record. The warm-down ride was quiet as Mike punched through the splits on the Garmin and mumbled something about the girl. How could she just turn up and put in a ride like that? Who was she? Shouldn't he have been told?

"Great ride Mike!" Old Dave Garner, the septuagenarian trike rider from Portsmouth North End CC, was the only one to speak as Mike made his way into the village hall to check the results. The embarrassed silence of the others should have told him all he needed to know, but when he looked up to the hand-written results on the tired old whiteboard, the small red letters broadcast his humiliation to everyone.

1. Alice Burbage - 17 mins 2.57 seconds (CR)

2. Mike Jarvis - 17 mins 10.82 seconds

He looked around to expectant faces. Smiling, he tried to hide his disappointment, but his voice, like the whiteboard, betrayed the undeniable truth.

"Where is she?"

"No one seen her Mike - she rode straight off the end of the course and away. No one seen her before." Only Dave had dared to speak.

Lily of the Valley

We'd always lived along the river bank. George liked it there because it was a calm and peaceful place. We'd been wandering up and down the banks of the River Lea for around ten years together and it felt like it was our home. People got to know George and many of them, despite his ragged appearance and motley collection of Sainsbury's bags and discarded bicycle bits, regarded him as a friendly face and a reassuring presence; he could fix punctures and do minor bike repairs for just a few pounds. He was known by a few of them as the 'Junkman'.

I was never sure where I came from except that George had picked me out of a skip somewhere in North Luton, near to the source of the Lea on Waulud's Bank; someone had cleared out a long-abandoned garage and I was left half-buried under an old sideboard. My memory of my previous life had been wiped after so many years in the darkness. When he got me and I awoke from my stupor, I realised that I was just a frame; but within half an hour, he'd added wheels and handlebars from his old bike - the frame on that one had broken due to the weight of his bags.

George never actually rode on me; I just carried the bags and he used my handlebars to lean on whenever he stopped for a chat or to watch a little blue Kingfisher darting along the river-bank. I know that George used to ride because I heard him talking to another old man about racing at the Paddington Cycle Track in the 1960's against that 'big bastard' Reg Harris; but now he was just content to walk. I don't know who Reg Harris was but George clearly didn't like him. In the summer months we would set up camp in Ware or Hertford and people seemed to get to know that we'd be there. Mothers used to come along with their children's bikes and wait patiently as George fixed them in the sunshine on the bank; pleasure cyclists would stop for a chat and a little adjustment here and there.

A few curious people had asked George about me in the past, but he'd brushed them away saying that I was just a piece of old scrap. It always hurt a bit when he said this; for some reason I felt I was better than just scrap - and I think he did too. OK, so I was found in a skip, but I was different to most other bikes; I had two wheels, a saddle and pedals like the others - although none of them matched - but inside, I felt different. I wasn't made of metal for a start. When George first found me he'd given me a coat of red paint and painted the name 'Lily' on my crossbar with a picture of a little flower after it. He said it was the best name for me because it reminded him of his ex-wife. He never said much about her but I think she left him for another cyclist; I often wondered if that was why he didn't give me any pedals. To stop me being ridden away like Lily.

But it all changed in the Olympic summer of 2012. That summer we'd wandered further south than we usually went and had watched the preparations for the Olympics in the Lee Valley Country Park where they had built the White Water adventure complex for the canoeists. We then continued even further south along the bank to where the A12 crossed the River at Hackney Wick. It was there that we saw the newly built Olympic Velodrome. George stood with me for ages and stared at the magnificent structure that seemed to have risen from the bare earth. He seemed a little upset as if remembering something from a long time ago; the future of British cycling was there in front of him; George was a small part of the past; he was one of the many club cyclists left trailing in the wake of Reg Harris, Britain's greatest post-war sprint cyclist. After gazing up at the elegant curves of the roof and the rounded cedar-clad ends, we turned around and walked back north again up the valley. Stopping for the night near the Lea Valley Marina, George lay awake, restless and grumpy, for ages. He was woken around seven by the sound of the rowers from the Lea Rowing Club on the opposite bank on one of their early Sunday morning outings. Unusually for him, George didn't move. He usually stood and saluted rowers whenever they paddled past. That day he just stared at the sky. It wasn't something he did.

Later that morning a man came along the path with a black dog; he was watching the river intently and didn't appear to see us camped under the shade of the trees until the last minute; George was sat motionless on the bank admiring the Yellow Flag irises on the opposite side and the purple Common Mallow flowers at his feet; I was leant against a large Ash tree. The dog bounded over towards us. Over the years George had learned how to be friendly to dogs and they came readily to the smelly old man with the willing scratch.

"Lovely dog, sir. Always love a Lab." The man turned, seeming a little surprised to see us, and stood and watched George with his dog; but he didn't speak. He was looking across our makeshift camp with a mixture of disapproval and intrigue. As George continued to play with the boisterous young dog he finally spoke.

"You staying here, mate?" It didn't sound threatening or aggressive but you never knew what people really mean when they speak.

"No sir - just passing through - I never 'stay' anywhere."

"Must get cold in the winter."

"You get used to it." George was always wary when he first met people. Over the years we'd had a few run-ins with unsavoury people who'd taken against us.

"You been on the road long?"

"Never been on the road, sir. Just stick to the river banks. About thirty five years, I think - I lose count, you know?" George gave his disarming smile.

"What's with the bike stuff?" George looked around at his assortment of tyres, rims and tubes hanging from my handlebars and the bags of assorted mechanical bearings and bits.

"Oh, well, I fix bikes if people want me to - you know, punctures and small things. Have you got a bike?"

"Yes - a few."

"Any need fixing?" The man smiled at the question.

"No, thanks, they're fine. Say, what's that bike there you got?" He was looking at me.

"It's just a pile of junk I pulled out of skip years ago - does me good for carrying stuff."

"Can I have a look at it?"

"Yeah - it's a bit scruffy - I painted her myself."

"I can see that. Lily - that's nice." The man knelt down next to me and tapped me gently with his fingernail. He raised an eyebrow at the dull hollow sound. Then he scratched a little at the red paint near my bottom bracket. Some of it chipped away easily revealing a small section of my black skin underneath.

"Hmm. Look, mate, I've got a bike at home that would be far better for what you need - it's not new, but it is a mountain bike with good thick tyres and a strong frame. Would you like a swap?"

"I've had Lily for years - she's been OK, but I've never ridden her. Why do you want her?"

"She's a bit like a bike I used to have when I was younger and I think I'd like to ride one like her again." George stared out across the river and sighed as if a weight had been taken from him. He hesitated.

"OK, if you want - but you'll have to show me the other bike first before we swap, mind?"

"No problem - how long will you be here?"

"Dunno. It's a nice day so I might stay another night. I'll just sit on the bank and watch the fish go by."

"Well, look, I'll be back this afternoon - can I bring you anything else - food, a jumper?" George smiled again.

"Always like food, sir - I'm easy, anything. Thank you sir."

Life changed very quickly after meeting the man. That afternoon my new owner took me away from the river in the back of his car after helping George swap his favourite cow-horn handlebars from me to the mountain bike. There was a rug laid out on the floor of the boot; he said that he didn't want me damaged. The following day I was taken to a bike shop where he and a mechanic stood and looked at me on a stand for about an hour and talked about me in hushed reverential tones. Then everything was stripped away from me, even my name and my paint were painstakingly removed - that took quite a long time. My old name was still there in big yellow letters underneath; Lotus. That night I did feel quite lonely hanging there in the workshop after everyone went home. There was no sound of the river bubbling past or George and his snores.

Three weeks later I was picked up by the man and we went back to his house where, again, he stood and stared at me for a long time. I had been given new wheels and a chain-set and some very strange handlebars. We did a short ride around the block where the man kept chuckling to himself like someone slightly mad.

Another week passed and we were sat on the start line of the F20/10 Time Trial course just outside Ware early on a sunny Sunday morning; Peter, dressed from head to toe in black lycra, smashed his PB on the 10 mile course that day. The comments from the starter, as we waited for the off on the line, made me realise just how special I really was.

"Someone said you had a new bike, Pete. But no one said you had a Lotus 110, like Boardman's Olympic bike - these are supposed to be rarer than hens teeth. Where did you get it from?"

Of Many Links Without a Break

"A fine day for a bicycle ride sir?" The friendly tone of the question didn't make Edward wish to reply.

Edward had stopped us at one of his favourite spots on the Wyche Road; we were half-way round one of our regular rides. The Malvern Hills provided a spectacular back-drop to our rides and could always be seen from his beloved Birchwood Lodge residence where he Alice stayed occasionally. We'd ridden this route many times and spoken to people we'd met but Edward wasn't in a conversational mood that day. The poor state of preparation that his new choral work was being subjected to by the orchestra chosen for the premiere - it was to be debuted in Birmingham in only a few weeks' time - had brought him down again. They just weren't good enough. Alice had been more than happy to see him take his sombre mood for a ride that late-Victorian summer afternoon; it would be only five months before their Queen, Victoria, was to pass away and an ominous tremor would encircle the earth; it was if he sensed that the world was about to change forever.

"E, dearest," she pleaded, as we were about to set off, "everything will be fine - the orchestra might not be the best, but they have another month yet. Go on, enjoy your ride with Mr Pheobus - everything will seem clearer when you return!" Mr Pheobus was the nickname he'd given me, although I had no idea why.

Edward smoothed his large moustache and finally looked, reluctantly, towards the eager, square-faced young man who'd pulled up alongside us on his own bicycle; Edward still didn't speak; E wasn't friendly at the best of times, and had been known to just ride away from people whose conversations he found tiresome.

"And that is a very fine bicycle sir - is it a Royal Sunbeam?" The young man had subtly detected E's disquiet at his presence but it just so happened that Edward was especially pleased with me, despite my very high price. He was more than happy to talk to someone who recognised the quality of his conveyance. I was bought on a whim the previous month and my £21/10/ price tag still sat heavily with his conscience; E felt I was an ostentatious luxury that his natural conservatism should have resisted; but he couldn't help himself in responding to this new line from his inquisitor.

"Thank you, young sir. It is a new acquisition and is lovely to ride - I can travel 80 miles in a day and not get tired - I feel very spoiled. I have named him 'Mr Phoebus'."

"As in Pheobus Apollo? - a very fitting name for such a handsome machine, sir!" E was slowly warming to our young companion who was similarly attired, but in tweed that was decidedly crumpled - and whose bicycle was distinctly inferior. He was clearly an educated young man.

"And what, young sir, brings you to this perfect place where all that can be heard is the sound of the summer wind in the trees?" E loved the supposed silence of the countryside. He spent at least three hours each morning orchestrating in his study with the window open to let the sights and sounds of nature in. 'It helps me to concentrate,' was his sharp response when Alice had questioned the draught from the open window.

"Me? Oh I just like to ride around the countryside - I'm a composer, you know. I'm always looking for old folk tunes for my collection. Are you from these parts sir? Do you know any folk tunes?" By now the young man had a notebook and pen in his hand as if expectantly waiting for E to begin. "If you can sing one then then I can write it straight down!"

I felt E's chuckle right down to my little oil bath. His mother had been a farm worker near Worcester before she'd married his musician father - E knew hundreds of folk tunes. E was a famous composer himself and this man didn't recognise him.

"Yes, a few." I knew that E felt that he was above the recent obsession for mere folk tunes as a basis for composition - he'd made the conscious decision to write music for the Empire; Victorian grandeur, prosperity, pomp and principles. Folk songs were not for E.

"Well, perhaps one day?..."

"Shhh..." Cut off in mid-sentence by the insistence of silence, he obediently followed E's sharp little eyes upwards to the sight of a small brown bird fluttering up messily from the open heath-land in front of us, towards the heavens. "Listen!"

The two of them stood motionless as the small brown lark burst into its characteristic song. Unusually, as it was mostly heard in the Spring, the melodious song burst high in the sky before floating away with the wind; the young man spoke first.

"Aha, the Lark Ascending - 'He rises and begins to round, he drops the silver chain of sound, of many links without a break, in chirrup, whistle, slur and shake'."

"George Meredith - beautiful words." They stood in silence again, before E continued. "The most memorable Folk songs always come from nature itself you know - these are the sounds and rhythms that we hear all our lives. There's music in everything if only men had ears."

"Yes, and were it not for the fact that I live in London, then I might hear them just a little more often." There was slight melancholy in his tone which was reciprocated by E.

"Ah, London, yes London. I too, young sir, am a composer and I too live mainly in London. In fact, I am currently writing a piece that is a musical portrait of our great capital city; it is, however, a portrait of the gluttony and drunkenness that the city revels in; the excesses of money and poverty laced with the poison of wine and the spirit of greed."

"So, a sort of cockaigne, sir?"

"Yes, exactly." E's voice trailed away and more silence ensued as the two of them gazing across from their vantage point at the green fields and hedgerows of the lush Severn Valley, digested the image of the spiritually empty, decaying city; a city that had entered the new century still revelling in the hedonistic certainty of an Empire that had ruled the world.

"A composer sir? Who, may I ask, are you?" E's shoulders visibly slumped and he looked to the young man with a genuine disappointment - hadn't the success of his Enigma Variations been broadcast to this young aspiring composer - where had he been for the past three years?

"My name is Edward Elgar." The young man's face suddenly beamed and he thrust his hand forward.

"Well, sir, who would have thought. It is such a great honour to have met you."

"And what is your name?"

"Ralph, sir. Ralph Vaughan Williams. But you'll not have heard of me. I'm just an organist and choirmaster in a small church in Lambeth. It's a thankless job but it does keep myself and my wife quite modestly."

"Well, it's been very nice to meet you - I must go now." Straightening his waistcoat and finely tuning the set of his bowler, E put his left foot on the pedal and scooted us along before carefully mounting the saddle and riding away. I watched the young man stare after us. His hand was raised as if to begin a wave; a wave which E wouldn't have returned even if he'd seen it. E was filled with excitement; the sound of that joyful lark rising so optimistically from the land had awakened something in him - he'd heard a new tune that would come but once in a lifetime; a tune so strong and so full of hope and glory that he, and it, would be remembered forever.

Blowing the lid off

The story of Dmitry and I in the forest ended, as it had begun, with a man stopping for a pee behind a tree. Tomorrow, the 26th of April, will be exactly thirty years from the day when Dmitry got hit on the head by that piece of concrete and fell down dead, right there, next to me. After the sound of the huge explosion that brilliantly lit up everything around us and silhouetted Dmitry against his chosen peeing spot, it all went very quiet again. The silence was brief and broken just a few seconds later, with the sound of debris raining through the leaves high above us. The piece of concrete that hit Dmitry was quite large; the 4 centimetre puncture hole still visible in the back of his skull probably explains why he died so quickly.

There's not much left of him now. His cratered skull sits stock-still, white and clean on the forest floor close by. Over the years, his flesh, bones and clothing have either disintegrated, sunk away into the soil, or been dragged away by scavengers. The crude lump of blackened concrete boiler lining sits, undisturbed, just a metre away.

It's been a bit lonely here and although I've come to like my tree, it's bark starting to envelop my cross-bar and its roots curling over the bottom of my wheels is a little perturbing. Lonely, that is, until this morning, when a van stopped beside the road and the man came into the trees near us; I was beginning to think that we would stay there, undiscovered, forever. Since the explosion I hadn't seen another living human being. Not for thirty years.

The day Dmitry died was strange in a lot of ways. Firstly, we were late to work. The two of us had been for a 100km ride earlier that day along the Vuzh River and, although he seemed content that his early season training was going well for that summer's races, the puncture in the last 10 kms meant we were delayed in getting back to the residential hall where he lived. He'd only fitted the new set of tubulars that morning and the roads had sped along beneath us in the crisp April air; until the loud popping sound from the rear tyre effectively ended the ride. Eventually arriving back, he'd refitted one of the old tubulars, sprinted to work and left me in the bike park just inside the perimeter road as per usual; before running hurriedly away to start his late shift, late.

Working the late shift meant he would usually be back to pick me up just after midnight but, for some reason, he was delayed; he had earlier talked to his neighbour about a routine test they were doing that evening, so I guessed that this could be why. In the event, he didn't come and unlock me until about 1.15 am; I became aware, quite quickly, that something untoward had happened because Dmitry was muttering under his breath as he knelt beside me whilst fumbling for the keys to the padlock; he never muttered - I only caught a few words.

"Damm…why didn't they tell me what went on in the briefing - I was only a few minutes late - how was I to know?" Standing up, and looking pensively back at the huge turbine hall, he continued,

"Why doesn't he listen to Aleksandr? He's the only one that has done this test before. Someone should report Dyatlov for the way he's been today - you can't treat fellow workers like that. Look, the test should have been aborted when the power fell to 30MW thermal. Something is wrong…. something is very wrong - it couldn't have been my fault."

Dmitry continued to grumble as we left the plant and headed out of the gate towards the road junction next to the Pripyat Monument. The air was very cold and the hundreds of high power lamps at the Power Station behind us lit our way on that darkest of nights. We had battery lights on the bike but the short ride to the town was usually so well-lit that we didn't need them. Stopping for a pee wasn't unusual for Dmitry - especially if we'd been for a ride earlier in the day. I think he drank too much strong coffee in the control room in an attempt to keep him alert and, as soon as we got going in the cold outside he frequently needed to stop on the way home. The junction was a favourite spot; it marked the entrance to the town of Pripyat with a three metre soviet-style stone carving of the town name with the year of its founding, 1970, underneath.

I was actually too good to be used as a bike for work, but the shortness of the commute and Dmitry's dislike of the bus meant that I was the only other option. Having been hand-built by Takhion in the capital, Kiev, a couple of years previously, my special Ishiwata tubing and Italian Campagnolo parts meant that I was similar in spec to the Russian national team bikes of the time - the fact that Takhion was named after Tachyon, the hypothetical sub-atomic particle that travels faster than the speed of light, was not lost on Dmitry. Such a pity we weren't able to travel that fast on that chilly afternoon after the puncture. Things might have been so very different.

The road next to the forest was very busy for a while after the explosion and hundreds of trucks and military vehicles trundled past on the road to the plant for many weeks. But then it went quiet again.

I'm not sure that I looked quite so special when I was found. My 'new' tubulars had largely fallen away from my wheels with only a few strips of fractured rubber left hanging in the breeze; my bar tape was dangling from my bars; my leather saddle was mildew green and swollen out of shape. The steel parts were still surprisingly clean and unblemished after thirty years in the forest - probably because there had been no scratches where the rain could have got through to the metal underneath and the trees had protected me from the sun's rays - but the alloy parts had dulled in the damp air.

It was the smell of his warm urine in the chilly air that took me back to the day of the explosion; he, the man with the van, was peeing against the same tree that Dmitry had done just before he'd died. As he finished, he turned, and I knew straightaway that he had seen me. He walked back, grasped my frame and grappled me away from the clutches of the tree and the roots before carrying me out, triumphantly, into the bright sunshine. Seeing the name on my down-tube he smiled and quickly put me in the back of the van before driving us away to the south.

We arrived at an apartment complex in West Kiev later that evening and he brought a man out to look at me lying messily in the back of the van on top of a pile of tools.

"I found it in the Chernobyl exclusion zone just outside the plant - must have been there since the reactor explosion in '86."

Cycle Schemer

I blanked out the last few minutes. I stopped listening when the muffled screams turned to choking just before the silence; but the two of them were still there behind the tree. Her pitiful pleas hushed in the cold and dark; I just froze. I'm usually stood upright when its dark, so it felt strange lying with my front LED's flashing aimlessly into the ground and my left pedal and handlebar grip sunk deep in the soggy turf; it seemed like she was begging him to stop right to the end.

The evening had started quite well. I was docked - anchored, as we call it - at the large rank on the south east corner of Hyde Park overlooking the Lanesborough Hotel where all the nice people stay. I'd only had two hires that day; firstly a Thai tourist lady, who thankfully, on account of her terrible cycling, only took me for a short but shaky tour around the Park for twenty minutes. Secondly, a lady from Liverpool who took me on a sedate pedal along Carriage Ride to gaze up at the Albert Memorial, and then back again. So quite nice for a cold, late September Wednesday. Around eight o'clock that evening, however, things changed.

Despite what people think, we Boris Bikes - as we've become known - live a pretty easy life. Most of our riders are either visitors or commuters; quite different in what they are out to achieve, but equally respectful of us; visitors try not to get themselves killed and commuters do their best to look after us. Every now and then we get taken by someone who treats us badly - one fool even rode one of us up Mont Ventoux in France! Some of us have been stolen and a few of us have even ended up at the bottom of the Thames; but mostly we just potter about town.

I knew that the man running obliquely from behind the darkened trees near the Holocaust Memorial Gardens in the middle of Hyde Park was wrong. Even through the gloom of the early evening, I could see he was running towards us and I just knew he was going to do something; my rider - a commuter man of around thirty, who I remember had taken me on this route across Hyde Park once before, didn't even seem to notice him - I think he was listening to Radio Four on his headphones. The hit was hard and the dull crunch resonated though my pressed steel frame as the running man's fist smashed into my rider's cheek. We crashed to the ground and my rider, who I initially thought had been knocked clean out by the punch, rolled onto his back in a slow motion daze with a moan and his dislodged earphones cackling with laughter; he was listening to *Just a Minute*, I think. I thought that would be it and we would be left there on the pavement. But it wasn't that simple. Our assailant came and stood over us and, after looking down at my rider for a moment, leant down, grabbed the leather satchel from his shoulder and emptied the contents onto the floor. He took a couple of things and then started to try to get into the inside pocket of the man's jacket; the man tried to stop him but, after another punch in the face, he lay still again. With the wallet now in his own pocket, the robber picked me up, casually adjusted my saddle up a bit and rode me away. He seemed very calm and rode me quite nicely up to Marble Arch, where, after deftly weaving his way through the busy evening traffic, we sauntered along Oxford Street.

As usual, the brightly lit shops were all still open and there were plenty of shoppers about; scanning the pavements I could tell he was looking for something. Suddenly he pulled me over near Bond Street tube station and he stood and intently watched the shoppers. Moving off again down Gilbert Street, I suddenly realised what was about to happen. Up ahead, close to the kerb, was a smartly dressed woman walking away from us with three or four shopping bags in her hand. We started to speed up and as we passed her, he put out his hand and simply took her shopping bags from her grasp without missing a pedal stroke - she didn't even have time to shout. A quick right - he didn't indicate - along Weighouse Street and then north again up Duke Street and we were back on Oxford Street. It was the easiest crime ever committed. After putting the contents of the bags into the rucksack on his back and throwing the carrier bags into a bin, we were off again.

Next was a man holding a woman with one hand and a shopping bag with the other. Easy, again - like plucking fruit from trees! A little while later, after we'd relieved several more unsuspecting shoppers of their bags, we met with a man near Marble Arch. He gave my rider a £50 note and we rode away. It all seemed so simple. I'd never been a getaway bike before; did it make me an accessory?

I thought that would be it, but it wasn't. We sped away from the lights and back to the darkness of the Park, heading out along North Carriage Drive. He was feeling hyper; hands too tight and legs too wayward. He was looking across to the path that ran on the other side of the grass and the trees growing alongside of the Drive. Again, I knew he was looking for something; like he knew there would be something there for him. The road was quiet with no one around. We may have been only yards away from the bustling Hyde Park Road that went from Marble Arch to Bayswater, but we could have been in the middle of nowhere; we were alone and the silence was ominous. He stopped, and still sitting with one foot on a pedal, he earnestly examined his mobile. I could hear the tiny beeps and dings as he answered texts and flipped through his Facebook. What were we waiting for?

I think I heard it first. Coming from behind us on the pathway behind the trees, I heard the sound of footsteps. Not just footsteps, but the regular scuffling sound of sneakers on autumn leaves; a late night jogger making a final sortie around the Park; people live the strangest hours in the centre of London. Then I saw her. She was tall and strongly built, wearing earphones and a tracksuit, and jogging slowly along the path towards us. I thought she had seen us, but her eyes were focused on the darkened pavement in front of her. He pretended not to notice as she passed us, no more than thirty feet away. As soon as she passed us he put his phone away and we started after her. Slowly, quietly, we crossed the grass strip and rode up behind her; he was picking his place and ensuring the coast was clear. Suddenly he accelerated and we were on her. He didn't bother to stop and just rode straight into her from behind. I crashed heavily on top of her as he jumped off at the last moment before grabbing her neck and punching her face. He dragged her by her hair from the path and into the darkness behind the nearest tree. I could hear it happening, but there was nothing I could do. I heard dull thumps and ripping sounds. She started to cry out but her voice was instantly muffled. She was clearly fighting for her life and, apparently, losing. It was horrible and I just looked at the ground, helpless. The moments of silence passed as drops of water from the recent rain ran freely into the grass from the small holes in my frame.

It could only have been a few minutes later that I was woken from my torment of guilt and horror by an eruption of noise and lights. Two police cars with blue lights ablaze slid to a halt with their headlamps blinding the scene. Peering through my spokes as they flickered in the lights, I saw her standing there next to the tree. She was not just alive; on his knees in front of her was my rider; handcuffed, his face beaten, and bleeding. Police Officer Meyer had got her man.

Marching in Tandem

"Monsieur President, sir, would you like to go for a ride with one of our girls?" The question being asked of Monsieur Woodrow Wilson did sound a little incongruous and, as he looked over at our little group, his face suggested he thought so too. But Marc, one of the Park Managers, hadn't meant anything untoward or immoral; it was a simple enquiry to see if the American President would like a ride around the Park on one of us tandems piloted by Clotilde or Irène; we'd been doing trips for the conference delegates for some weeks since they'd all arrived in Versailles. The wide open spaces and the fresh air of the beautifully manicured Palace Park had come as a welcome relief for some of the representatives from overseas who'd spent many long hours in meetings and deliberations over the Peace Treaty they were there to finalise; I also think that some of them also liked the idea of sitting on the back of a tandem being supervised by a pretty young French girl. One of the Italian ministers, who'd clearly taken the invitation to mean something else, had received a sharp rebuke from Clotilde for refusing to keep his hands on the handlebars.

I had seen Monsieur Wilson pacing up and down at the back of the Palace a few times over the past weeks - he was usually in deep conversation with his closest adviser, Monsieur Edward House - but today he was alone and seemingly a little melancholy. On seeing the two girls stood prettily alongside us tandems, his stiff, slightly gloomy, demeanour changed quite markedly; a handsome man with square features, he cracked a pleasant smile that revealed a charming, if not playful, person; an informality that would have been somewhat out of place at the negotiating table.

"Well I don't think I would mind if I did! - I have seen these contraptions back home in the United States, but I have never ridden on one." I could see quite quickly that he had singled out Irène for his pilot; she was the more placid of the two girls with the slightly larger and fuller figure; a stoutish frame much closer, I was later informed, to that of his young wife, Emily. Clotilde, on the contrary, was angular and bony with her elbows as sharp as her tongue - as the Italian delegate had discovered. Her face frequently expressed a sneer; Monsieur Wilson could read people well.

Madame Emily Wilson was one of the few wives of the foreign dignitaries that had come with their spouses to the talks, and it became well-known that she was taking the opportunity to spend her days shopping in the upmarket Parisian stores that still managed to sell their high quality goods - despite the war being barely over and the streets still filled with de-mobbed soldiers begging for change. If not shopping, she would be playing her favourite game at the nine-hole Golf de l'Ermitage course on the outskirts of the City. It may have been the first time that a serving American President had ever been to Europe but, in spite of the importance of the task confronted by her husband and the other leaders to negotiate a settlement after an interminable four years of war, she wasn't going to miss the chance to enjoy herself.

"Would you like a cigarette before the ride Monsieur Wilson?" Marc held out a languid hand with an open silver cigarette holder for the President. Wilson's jaw hardened slightly as he looked dismissively at the offering.

"No thank you sir - I think my Father did enough smoking in his life for the both of us."

"Sir, Mr President?" Just as Monsieur Wilson was about to climb on the seat behind Irène, another, younger and bespectacled man, hurried towards us from the direction of the Palace. "Sir, do you have a moment?" I sensed a large sigh and a touch of annoyance from Monsieur Wilson; it seemed that just as he'd discovered a moment's escape from the incessant negotiations, his attention was being demanded of again.

"Yes, but only for a moment - what do you want?" He was quite firm and short towards the earnest young man who, I think, immediately realised that his target wasn't happy with the prospect of more talking, so quickly changed tack.

"Sir, why don't I join you on the other bicycle? I take it you are taking a spin around the Park? We could talk as we ride together." Despite his dexterous change of direction, the man's English accent and straight words suggested he wasn't a politician; but he was definitely charming. Monsieur Wilson seemed to calm a little.

"That would be fun, sir - sorry, what was your name again?"

"Keynes, sir, John Keynes."

"Yes, of course that is who you are, my apologies - your Prime Minister, Mr George Lloyd speaks very highly of you. So are you ready for this? Quickly, let's get going before someone else comes." There was a slightly childish thrill to Monsieur Wilson's tone as if he was pleased to be getting away from it all, even if only for a few minutes joyride to chat with the bright young economist from Great Britain.

It was clear from the start that Monsieur Wilson wasn't as fit as Keynes, and his partnership with Irène was always going to be a little cumbersome, but our two teams rode together through the near-deserted formal gardens of the Parterre de Latone and onto the Allee Royal. The crisp chill of the March air was softened by the low sun that shone as brightly as it could on the brilliantly coloured tulips, narcissi and hyacinths that bordered our ride and which contrasted with the grey and unbroken surface of Grand Canal lying just ahead of us in the centre of the Park; the early morning frost had lifted and the paths were smooth and safe under our silky pneumatic tyres. Nobody spoke for the first few minutes as they accustomed themselves to their machines and the peculiar proximity of their partners. I felt that Monsieur Wilson was quite comfortable in his seat but, looking at Monsieur Keynes, I sensed an unease as he sat as far back as the saddle would allow; I don't believe he was used to the presence of women. Irène and Clotilde ensured that we rode alongside each other closely and the two girls exchanged knowing glances and furtive smiles; who'd have thought that they would have been riding tandems through le parc du Chateau Versailles with the President of the United States aboard; that most powerful man, who, after sending his soldiers to bring to an end the dreadful war, had sailed triumphantly from America to assist with the peace.

"So, young man, what was it you wanted to ask?" Monsieur Wilson was clearly beginning to relax into the ride and was calming down a little from whatever had upset him earlier.

"Well, sir, I just wanted to talk, if I may, about Germany?" Monsieur Wilson thought for a moment.

"Well, that is why we're all here after all."

"Sir, if I may… I just wanted to say that I think that it is important that your proposals should be presented a little more forcefully to my Prime Minister and the French Prime Minister, Monsieur Clemenceau. I have been trying to suggest that Mr Lloyd George relaxes our stance on the German reparations - but it seems that he has changed his view since we left London - he keeps pressing for larger and larger sums. It is my belief, sir that elements of your own 14 point plan will genuinely make for a better economic future for Europe."

"In what way?"

"Well, it seems to me that what Mr Lloyd George and Monsieur Clemenceau are proposing is the most outrageous act of cruelty by the victors over a defeated nation that has ever been seen in civilised society. It is a Carthaginian Peace. Everyone in London and Paris wants Germany to pay for the war, but the amounts they are talking about will skin her alive for year after year into perpetuity. My hypothesis is that the only way to build a proper peace is for us to re-build Germany into a better society with a sound financial footing. We, the victorious nations should be doing so much more than simply exacting revenge." Monsieur Wilson paused for a moment before replying.

"You may be right, and whilst I am in agreement with you, it would seem your Prime Minister is only doing what his electorate wants and Clemenceau is seeking nothing more than revenge for the Franco-Prussian war that cost the French people so dearly half a century ago."

"I know that sir. But I believe I am with a Government that is working for ends I think are criminal."

"Those are strong words. Are you sure Mr Keynes?"

"Yes, completely. And you, sir, are in the best position to broker the situation for everyone - the United States is the biggest creditor and you have helped to close out the war. If you were to right-off America's loans to Germany then it would at least show intent. We shouldn't be crushing Germany - there will be repercussions you know; vengeance doesn't limp!"

We rode on in silence for a while with just the sound of the spokes whirring through the air and the girls' crisp linen culottes flapping with the speed. At the end of the Allee Royale, Irène waved to Clotilde to get her attention.

"Nous irons a gauche et vous allez a droite?" Clotilde nodded with a little Gallic smile as we parted and circled the huge oval pond in opposite directions. Called Bassin d'Apollon, the low walled pool features the huge bronze centrepiece depicting the Greek god Apollo rising from the sea on a four-horse chariot.

As we passed each other at the top of the pond, Monsieur Keynes called out to the President.

"It's in your hands sir - the future of Europe is in your hands - don't forget that the seed of revolution is repression!"

After circling the pond once more we headed north up the Allee Saint Antoine to the junction with the Avenue de Trianon. There we stopped with our breathless guests and walked along the grassy border with its crocussed carpets.

"John, I do agree with you - I have been discussing with your Prime Minister and Clemenceau about the size of the payments that they want - and I too believe that we should be strengthening democracy by self-determination of the peoples of Europe - not trying to teach them a lesson."

"Germany is no longer a people and a state; it has become a mere trade concern being placed by its creditors into the hands of the receiver." The two of them were walking slightly ahead of Irène and Clotilde, but we could still hear them as their voices rose with the strength of their convictions.

"…John, you need to know that I could never get the Senate to agree to writing down the debt. Look, I understand entirely your belief but no one knows what will happen tomorrow. I came to Paris with a plan to realise a vision, to realise an ideal - to re-discover liberty among men. But the complications of the people of Europe are far worse than I ever imagined. There is no will to live together and help each other."

At that moment they were interrupted by the sound of hoarse coughing; Irène was leant over my handlebars and convulsing painfully.

"What is wrong Irène?" asked Clotilde without moving towards to her colleague. Irène shook her head. She suddenly looked very pale. Monsieur Wilson came over to us and, with a genuinely paternal touch, placed his hand on her forehead as she looked dolefully up at him.

"You are very hot - chaud? - you have a fever! Come, we must take you back. With his arm around the fast fading Irène, he walked her gently back to the rear of the Palace as Monsieur Keynes and Clotilde followed behind pushing us tandems. At the Palace Irène was helped indoors by a clearly embarrassed Marc. The two of us were left leant against the wall close to the two men as Clotilde followed her stricken friend inside.

"She didn't look well at all - it was a genuine fever - and it came on so quickly with the cold air and the exertions of the ride." There was a palpable bleakness in Monsieur Wilson's voice.

Irène died as the clock struck eight that evening. The flu epidemic that had decimated the soldiers in the war-torn trenches to the north during the previous summer had, by then, spread to the civilian population and had claimed another victim. The Spanish flu, as it was known, appeared to attack the young and healthy more so than the old and the weak; the immediacy of chills, fever and fatigue took them down within hours. We heard later that Monsieur Wilson too, was struck down, within a day; probably breathing in Irène's infected air. He survived, but the enforced time away from his work at the Conference, however, ensured that Monsieur Clemenceau (or 'Pere la Victoire' as he was nicknamed by the French Press) got his way and he 'skinned' the German people; the British, too, squeezed the German lemon until the little pips squeaked.

Clemenceau was old at the time of the Peace Conference of 1919, so didn't live to see the vengeance wrought by the people he had made pay for the tragedies of the Somme, of Verdun, and of Passchendaele. Monsieur Keynes resigned his post shortly after his meeting with the President when his pleadings were ignored by his Prime Minister. The future might have been so very different if we'd not taken that ride in the Park.

About the Author

Simon Bever is originally from Portsmouth but has spent most of his life in London. He graduated from Goldsmiths College with a music degree, and after working in the financial services and data marketing industry's, he is now co-founder of the online cycle accessory retailer, pedal-pedal.co.uk. He owns and rides plenty of bicycles.

Other books by Simon A. Bever;

The Artless Dead; Set in the theatres and concert halls of London in 2010, The Artless Dead is about 15 theatrical and musical performances and introduces the reader to a group of regular theatre goers and music lovers. From Bach to the Beatles and Shakespeare to Stoppard, love blossoms, lives are lost and hidden secrets are revealed beneath the modern suburban civility.

Beware of the Cats; The lions of Serengeti Park are starting to hunt humans. The perfect storm of political ineptitude, global weather changes and the gradual movement of man into the plains had started a change that will create the biggest human disaster to occur in thousands of years. For Trent Darnell and his two friends on their motorbike trip through Africa, the changes in the Serengeti will change their lives forever.

Eye of the Needle; The seemingly excessive criminal damage to a sports car on the Embankment one muggy evening rush hour is the precursor to a series of increasingly violent events from an unknown perpetrator. A quiet young PC is slowly embroiled in the tense re-enactment of a conflict from the ancient past and the race is on to catch or be caught. There are unseen powers at work in this riveting tale and help comes from the least expected quarters.

Spanish Castle Magic; She thought she had everything sorted with her advertising job in Central London, her flat and her tall handsome boyfriend. But something was missing in her life and she knew what it was. A celebration party for one married couple, ended up with the break-up of another; a catalyst that would change everything for Sara and the people who were there.

21574438R00074

Printed in Great Britain
by Amazon